Monica's

Outlaws

Patricia Murphy

PARTRIDGE
A Penguin Random House Company

To order additional copies of this book, contact
Toll Free 800 101 2657 (Singapore)
Toll Free 1 800 81 7340 (Malaysia)
orders.singapore@partridgepublishing.com

www.partridgepublishing.com/singapore

INTRODUCTION

The is a western about four men and one woman.
They were very dangerous as they did whatever they wanted
and it looked as if no one could stop them.

But there was one man who was going to try. He had a very
good reason to want to see them behind bars.
Two others had their own reasons for wanting to find these
outlaws and bring them to face justice.

But Monica and her gang were not going to make it easy for
anyone who tried to bring them down.
They rode hard and fast to stay one step ahead of the law

ABOUT THE AUTHOR

This is Patricia's third book; her first two books were for children. They are titled "Tanya's Adventure's" and "Percy the owl and friends"—Here she tries her hand at an adult book and hopes you enjoy it.

CHAPTER 1

The Hunt

A tall stranger came down out of the mountain. This man was on a special mission. He was there to find the evil bunch who murdered his entire family.

There were five of them one woman and four men ridding on to the North ranch. Jake was in the barn seeing to the animals.

His father asked five strangers to come in and have breakfast. Everything seemed fine then all hell broke loss.

Jake heard his mother and sister scream, then he heard shots fired.

He wanted to go help them but knew there were too many of them. There was nothing he could do.

Jake stayed in the barn and watched for them to leave. He made sure he got a good look at them as they came out of the house.

The woman was what they call a half-breed she was half-Indian and half-Spanish. Jake heard one of the men call by Name it was Monica.

Monica was beautiful woman with long black hair that hung all the way down her back. Her eyes were green and her skin was very dark.

There was something different about her. She had long strong looking finger nail that were longer than most. She could slit your throat with them they weapons. Monica was the worst

1

of the five she was cold with a heart of stone that made even the men fear her.

One of the men who ran with Monica was a very large strong black man. His name was Sammy and he had arm like tree trunks. He could snap a person's spine like a twig.

Another was Phillip the French-man he loved alcohol it did not matter if it was whiskey or rum or whatever as long it was alcohol.

He thought of himself as a lady s man until he got fed up with them or they did not do what he wanted when that happened, he would slap then around but sometimes times he went too far and would hurt them so badly he killed them.

Then there was Anton, the dirty little Mexican. He stood about five-feet tall in his stocking feet.

Anton looked like he did not know what water and soap was his hair was long dirty and hung all over his face.

The only thing he was good for was that he knew how to handle a bowie knife he never missed his target

Last was Harold the English man he was a man of much knowledge of many things specially was explosives. He was tall, thin, and blond-haired with blue eyes. Harold did not say much he let his actions speak for him.

The outlaws were sitting around a table playing cards in the trading post.

As usual they were all cheating each other. Monica said "come on you guys I've had enough of this place. It's time to get out of here and have some real fun." "Oh yeah and do what?" Sammy asked "I'll let you know on the way now are you coming or not?"

As they rode west Monica told them of a small farm where they could have a lot of their kind of fun. "That's more like it yahoo" Sammy yelled.

Jake had been in the saddle all day both he and his horse needed a rest.

He found a good place to make camp for the night and stopped it did not take long before he had a pot of coffee brewing and put some bacon and beans on the fire.

A sudden movement in the bush behind made him jump up and draw his gun.

"Come out or I'll shoot". A tall stranger stepped out and said. "No, don't shoot I'm harmless boy that coffee sure smells good."

Jake could see from the way the man dressed that he was from another country.

Jake looked the man up and down then asked. "What the hell are you doing out here where is your horse and gear?"

"Sir can I get near the fire first, I am rather cold you know?". Jake motioned the man to sit by the fire and shared dinner and coffee. "Here this will warm you up you can't be too careful out here" Jake told him.

The stranger told Jake that his name was Albert Jenkins and that he was a police officer from London. He said he was looking a criminal who was wanted back in England for murder."

"So where is your horse" Jake asked again. Oh that blighter threw me a ways back and I have been on foot since

The next morning Jake told Albert that he knew of a farm nearby where he would be able to get another horse.

But Albert was not in any hurry to move on. "come on Albert we need get started" "sir you have the advantage over me" Albert said. "how so" Jake asked. "Well you know my name but I do not know yours." "Oh is that all I can fix that right now I am Jake North and I too am on the trail of some killers."

They rode together on Jakes horse up to the Wilcox ranch. As they got close to the front door Beth came out holding a double-barrel shot gun. "That's far enough" she called out. "Hey Beth it's me Jake North" Jake called back to her.

Beth lowered the gun and came a little closer to them and said "Ah Jake come in."

As Jake and Albert walked into the house Beth whispered to Jake *who is the dude you have with you?* "Beth I want you to meet Mr Jenkins he's from England."

He is out here looking for a criminal wanted for murder in England.

It was about lunchtime so Beth set out lunch and they sat around talking for a while.

Then she took them out to the stables to get Albert a horse.

Beth handed Jake a sack with food in it and said" Here you make sure you come back for a visit one day and take care" "Thanks Beth I will."

Later that day Jake asked Albert "do you have a wanted poster of your man, the man you are hunting down?" Albert pulled an old paper from his pocket and showed it to Jake.

Jake looked at it for a long time then said "yes I've seen this man. He is running with a bad bunch" "Then you won't mind if I ride along with you" Albert asked. "No not at all it will be good to have some company"

Jake and Albert rode for a long while and saw there was no sign of the outlaws It was getting dark so they stopped and made camp for the night.

The next day the evil ones rode to the Mitchell's farm Monica banged on the door. "I thought we were going to have some fun it looks like we rode all this way for nothing" Sammy said

Monica got so angry she went over to Sammy, pulled him of his horse and said "if you want to keep on breathing keep your big yap shut."

With that Sammy just sat on the pouch along with the rest of them and waited.

It was not long before the Mitchell family came home.

Jack stopped the wagon at the steps and helped his wife and baby down.

The other two children got down by them self.

Jack turned to his family and said "come on we have visitors. We must welcome them."

Beryl went over to Monica and invited them into their home for lunch.

Marty and Billy stood by their father and watched. They did not know what to make off these people things did not seem to be right somehow.

The two boys ate their lunch and both went outside to the barn. Billy dragged his younger brother in to the barn so he could talk to him.

"Marty I don't trust this lot. They look bad to me. No matter what you hear I want you to hide in the hay-loft you hear me" "yes but why" "don't ask questions Marty, just do as I say" Billy said sure that things were going to go terribly wrong.

Jack brought out a jug of corn liquor and that was when all hell broke loose.

Monica told her men "I don't care what you lot do, but if anything happens to that lovely baby you will have to answer to me understood."

Sammy just had to push her buttons one more time. "Yeah what you have in mind for the little one?"

"That is none of your concern I swear Sammy sometimes you go too far questioning my moves"

By this time the outlaws were good and drunk but the liquor had run out and there was no more.

Monica asked Beryl. "Can I help you with those dishes?" "Thank you it is nice to get help now and again."

The dishes were all most done when the baby started to cry. "I'll take care of her okay Beryl?" "Oh yes It's nice having another woman around for a change."

Monica picked up the baby walked around the house for a while, and then outside for a walk that they were not going to come back from.

Harold said to the others very quietly "Monica left. Now the fun begins Sammy you find those two brats and deal with them. We don't want any-one telling tales."

Billy heard this and started towards the barn. "Marty Run, run fast and get away" he called out.

Marty heard him and scrambled though a hole in the back wall of the barn and kept running until he could run no more He found a heap of bushes to hind in.

Billy ran into the barn with Sammy hot on his trail he grabbed a pitch fork and threw it at Sammy it caught him in the leg and Sammy fell.

Billy took off in the same direction as Marty had.

He called out, but not so any-one could hear him except Marty "come out Marty It's me I'm a-lone"

Marty heard Billy and came out of hiding "oh Billy what are we going to do now where are we going to go?" "one thing at the time Marty we are a-live and that is the main thing"

Billy found a place for him and Marty to stay for the night. He thought it would be all right for them to go back to the house in the morning.

The next day they went back and Billy told Marty to wait a bit up the road a piece while he checked everything out.

He found what he expected his father and mother were dead he took their bodies out the back and buried them.

After rounding up some of their things he set off to get Marty and go into town to find someone to help them.

Monica took the baby to Indians she knew who bough young white babies and children and used them as slaves when they grew big enough.

It was getting dark when Jake and Albert rode up to the Mitchell Farm.

The front door was wide open Jake thought this was very odd so he went in very carefully. Albert said "hey Jake there is no sign of life anywhere."

By this time Jake was out back staring at the two freshly dug graves. Albert came up behind him and said. Now I can see why. "There are only two graves out there I wonder where the children are?" Jake asked. "Maybe they got to safety." He put his hand on Alberts shoulder and said "I pray to god they did. Come on we best be on our way."

In town the boys headed straight for the sheriff's office to get help.

As luck would have it the sheriff's wife was there and saw that the boys were tied. "Oh you poor things you come along with me I will take care of you and you can talk to my husband later."

After riding for a while Albert saw that Jake had something on his mind he had not said a word since leaving the Mitchell farm.

"I say old bean what has got you so quiet?" Albert asked "I have been thinking about the baby the Mitchell's had a few weeks ago and the two boys.

What happened to them there were only two graves.

Jake puzzled. "Maybe the boys took the baby with them and they are all safe." "yeah maybe" Jake was not so sure.

The outlaws meet up with Monica just outside a small town named Riverview.

They sat on the banks of the river making plans about what to do next. Sammy's leg was giving him some pain and he was moaning so much it was getting on every ones nerves

"Oh Monica can't you do something about him" Harold complained.

"Yeah cut it off and he would have nothing to whine about" Anton said holding up his bowie knife.

Monica had enough of their yapping "I'll into town and see if I can get a doctor for him you stay put."

Phillip wanted to go to town to find some ladies and something to drink. "To hell with sitting around here I'm bored let's make our own fun, anyone coming with me"

"Yeah me I'm sick of just sitting" Anton said as he stood up.

When Monica came back with the doctor, she was not happy about the missing me.

The doctor looked at Sammy's leg and he did not like what he saw. "This leg is infected and I will have to lance it. But you will need someone to hold him down while I do it."

Monica jumped on Sammy's chest and Harold got hold of his legs and the doctor went to work on Sammy's leg with a knife it hurt so much Sammy screamed real loud.

The doctor was only half way finished when Sammy passed out. That made it a bit easier and Monica Harold could let go.

When the doctor had finished he wrapped the leg with a clean bandage and said "Now keep the bandage clean and change the dressing every day and you just might save his leg."

Monica thanked the doctor and paid him. After the doctor left she turned her attention to the missing men. "Now Harold where are those other bastards."

"I think you can guess where they are" "yes in town well they won't be for long"

Monica took off into town leaving Harold to baby-sit Sammy.

Sammy started to come around and said "hey what happen to my leg?" "Stay still you are not to move the doctor worked on it but you have to rest" Harold told him.

Jake and Albert were a few miles out of town when it suddenly dawned on Jake where the children may have been taken.

"Oh no I hope I am wrong but sometimes children are sold to the Indians" Jake said "she would not do that would she they are not that bad are they?" Albert asked.

"You bet your sweet life she would the Indians pay top dollar for white children. When they get old enough they use them as slaves" Jake told Albert.

Anton and Phillip were having themselves a good time. They had found some willing girls and were up stairs in one of the rooms.

Monica walked into the saloon and asked the bar man if he had seen a Frenchman and Mexican "yes they are up stairs."

When Monica was half way up the stairs she could head a lot of crying and screaming coming from one of the rooms.

One of the ladies came out of the door but Anton grabbed her before she could get away.

Monica pushed the door open and that took them by surprise "What the hell are you doing?" she yelled "shut that bloody door" was the answer she got from Anton. He did not know it was Monica standing behind him.

Monica looked around the room and there was blood everywhere. One of the ladies was dead and the other one was dying.

"Now that you two have had your fun, get your ass back to the river and I'll clean up your mess as usual."

Both men turned around saw that it was Monica they just left the room.

Back at the river Monica told them that if anything like that happens again she would kill them "we don't any want trouble. And I thought I told you men not to go into town" "Yeah and who died and made you boss" Anton asked. Monica grabbed him by the throat and pressed her long sharp nails into him until she drew blood "now what did you say about who is the boss."

"Umm . . . . nothing . . . . you're boss."

Monica let him go and said "Glad we got that settled."

Jake and Albert rode into town from the south end of town and did not see the outlaws

Jake told Albert about a hotel at the end of the street. He said "you will get rooms there and I'll meet you there after I see the sheriff."

When Jake got to the sheriff's office he found the sheriff a sleep in his chair.

Jake made a loud bang on the desk that made the sheriff jump to his feet. "What the hell! Better yet who are you and what do you want lad?"

Right then the barman from the saloon came in And said. "Sheriff there has been a killing at my saloon" the barman Frank yelled.

"Wait your turn Frank this lad was here first" "Now boy what is it you wanted" "I want report a mass murder" Jake reported. "All right boy let me get some details" Jake told the sheriff about the outlaws who murdered his family. "Okay lad I'll look in to it as soon as I can"

Jake felt like he was just patted on the head and sent away *"yeah sure you will sheriff"* he thought to himself as he walked to the hotel.

Albert was waiting for him on the steps "well what did the sheriff say?" "Not much the lazy old coot."

"But I did find out that there was a killing in the saloon I think I should talk to the barman" Jake said.

Jake and Albert walked into the bar and the barman asked "what will it be boys?" "Whiskey and some answers" Jake said.

What kind of answers are you looking for pal" Frank asked.

Jake and Albert had a long talk to Frank about the outlaws but Frank did not know who did the killings.

Early the next morning Jake was awakened by a woman calling out for help.

He went to the window and saw a lady in a buggy with a man slumped over the front seat.

Albert was all-ready up and dressed he went down stairs "hi what has happened here?"

The lady responded-"This is Robert Buckingham my husband. He needs a doctor fast."

By this time Jake was there looked at the man and said "sorry madam this man is long gone a doctor cannot help him I'm sorry for your loss"

Albert took the lady into the hotel and the maid got her a strong cup of tea.

Jake went into the hotel to ask her some questions. "Hi ma'am my name is Jake North and this man here is Albert Jenkins he is from London and he is hunting a criminal that is wanted for murder."

"I am also looking the outlaws that killed my whole family." She told them "My name is Kate Buckingham I know just who you are looking for they are called Monica's gang."

"They roam around doing whatever they want and no one can stop them" She told them. "Well Kate we are here to say we will bring them to justice" Albert said.

They left Kate at the hotel and headed for the stables to saddle up and strap their packs onto their horses.

Suddenly someone was standing at the door of the stables. Albert eyes widened and his mouth dropped open.

Jake looked around he saw Kate standing there dressed in jeans, a shirt, and she had guns strapped around her waist. They were tied down like a gun fighter.

"I'm coming with you", she said. "The trail is no place for a lady you will be better off staying here" Albert said. "Albert shut your mouth and you can stop staring"

"I told you my name was Kate Buckingham. Five years ago it was Kate Watt's maybe you have heard of me. I got married and stopped fighting other people's wars."

"Yes I have heard of you and I think you will be a great help you know all about this country and it-s people."

CHAPTER 2

The killings

Monica and her gang had came to a this small house about five miles out of town.

It was a lovely little house with a white fence a flower garden in the front, and a vegetable garden in back.

They rode up to the back of the house and left the horses tied up to the back fence.

Monica walked up to the back door a grey-haired old lady saw her coming.

She opened the door just a bit she had a small gun in her hand in her dress pocket.

"Yes what do you want?" she asked "I'm looking for a Mrs Nancy Wicker I have something for her." "Oh yes what is it?"

Monica stepped real close to Nancy.

That is far enough "Nancy said as she pulled out the gun from her pocket" back of or I will shoot."

Monica saw that Nancy meant what she said so she turned around and started to walk away.

Suddenly Monica turned pulled her gun real fast and shot Nancy.

Nancy fell and was dead before she hit the floor with a bullet in the middle of her forehead.

Monica's men were around the front when they heard the shot they barged in the door with their guns drawn.

Nancy's husband Bob told his young granddaughter to run to her room and lock herself in.

Phillip followed the girl to her room and said" ah come on don't be like that you know a locked door is not going to stop me. Make it easy on yourself and open the door there is a good girl."

Phillip told her. But Fay was not going to open the door" no go away I know what you want and you will not get it from me I would rather die first."

By now Phillip's was getting angry so he put all of his might to the door and forced his way in.

Fay had one choice and that was to climb out the window. She was half-way out when Phillip grabbed her by the leg and drug her back in.

Phillip pushed her on-to the bed, pinned her by the arms to the bed with one hand and with the other he ripped the front of her dress till it came wide open.

Fay twisted and turned till she broke loose from his grip and ran to the door.

He stopped her again, grabbed her by the hair and held her dead in her tracks.

"You little bitch get your ass on that bed I am going to do things you never have dreamed of I will put you on cloud nine."

While Phillip was having his way with Fay Monica and the others were sitting around drinking the whiskey they found in a cupboard.

They had shot Bob and left his body in the hallway where he fell." Come on Phillip hurry up we want to get out of here" Sammy called out.

Monica wanted to get going before someone so she went to the girl's room when she got close she could hear Fay screaming.

Then there was no sound so Monica went in Phillip was still putting his cloth's on.

Monica whipped his ass and said" come on we are moving it is not safe to hang around too long. You made a mess of her is she dead?" "ah Monica you know I don't leave anyone to tell tales."

Jake Albert and Kate were on their way out of town a few miles down the track they came to an old house. Kate let out an al-mighty scream" oh my goodness it is still standing I don't believe it." "What don't you believe?" Albert asked.

"That is the house I grew up in" "we have a bit of time to spare if you want to take a look around" Jake said.

When they got close to the back fence they heard a voice call for help from inside the house. "Kate you stay here Albert and I will check it out."

In the house they found the awful mess that Monica and her gang left behind. In one of the rooms they saw a young girl when she saw the two men she started to scream loud and curl up on the bed.

"Jake I think it would be better if Kate handled this you know woman to woman." "Yeah you may be right."

Albert went outside and called to Kate "Kate there is a young girl inside and she needs help."

When Kate went into the room what she saw made her feel real sick. "Hi there my name is Kate, I want to help you will you let me?" Kate said trying to make the girl feel at ease.

Then the Girl said "My name is Fay Hollings, the other people out there are my grandparents are they all right?"

"Why don't we get you cleaned up first" Kate said.

When Kate did all she could for Fay she took her to the living room.

Albert came over to her and said "miss there was nothing we could do for your family I am sorry."

Jake came in from getting ready to bury Fay's grandparents "everything is ready" he announced.

After they buried the dead had to find a place for Fay to stay so they took her back to town.

By this time it was late so they decided to stay in town and leave in the morning.

The next day the three of them set off again

"Kate do you have any more houses you grew up in" Albert asked with a wide grin on his face.

Kate looked at him and answered "smart ass as a matter of fact as I grew up all over the place I don't know what might happen next."

She said it with the same grin on her face

"If you two are finished swiping at each other we better get a move on. We need to find somewhere to bed down for the night" Jake broke in.

They found a good place for a camp near a river Albert and Jake set up the fire and put coffee on.

Kate washed up and cook their dinner while the others washed up.

The next day they rode for a very long time and finally came up on an Indian camp.

They looked friendly enough but Jake was careful "let me talk to the chief stay on your guard."

So they rode in very slowly and found the old chief sitting outside a tepee. Jake got down off his horse and stood in front of the chief.

"Hi there" he said.

"While Jake was talking to the chief Kate saw an Indian lady with a white baby in her arms." "Albert that could be the Mitchell's baby" she said very quietly. "Yes maybe but don't say anything now we'll tell Jake later we don't want to start anything we can't finish's."

Jake left the chief walked back to the other two waiting for him and said "We need to get the hell out of here fast."

There was no time for questions they jumped on their horse and rode hard and fast.

The Indians were close behind them whooping and hollering Jake knew that Forte Ute was nearby so they headed for it.

When the Indians saw where they were going they broke off and went back to their camp.

After the dust settled Albert asked "now would you kindly tell me what that was all about my good man?"

"Yes I will tell you. But when I say do not say anything I mean it. A young brave heard what you said about the white baby and told the chief."

"Well what are you going to do about the white baby? You can't just leave it there to be their slave" Albert asked.

"First of all pal; we have time on our side. For now she is only a baby. But now I'm going to talk to the colonel."

Colonel Mayberry came out of his office and greeted Kate "lovely to see you again have you come to see your Aunty Mavis?"

"Umm not just yet uncle we need to talk to you. Can we go into your office?"

In the office Kate introduced her Uncle to Jake and Albert and told him about Monica and her gang. "Then she said now I will go see Aunty Mavis and let you men talk."

Kate went to see her Aunty Mavis who came to greet her "Katie my dear it has been a long time."

She gave Kate a great big hug took her inside for a cup of tea and a long awaited talk to catch up with everything.

Albert told the colonel "sir we saw a white baby in that Indian camp I would like to go in and get her out."

"No son we don't do things like that here. We leave things as they are."

"But colonel we just can't leave her there. She will be made their slave when she gets old enough" Albert argued.

Jake butted in "Albert we would do more harm than good. She has been theirs for a while she is theirs now let it go."

But Albert would not let it go "but you said we had time on our hands we must be able to do something"

"Albert I was wrong. As the colonel said it is too late and these Indians are different. They will raise her as their own now let it rest okay" Jake warned.

Albert went outside and started to kick the dirt.

Kate saw him went over to him and said "No luck with the Colonel huh? the baby stay's where she is."

"Yes how did you know oh let me guess your Aunty. Everyone knows everything about this place I am beginning to get that now."

As it was Friday night and the Forte al-ways had a dance so Kate asked Albert to come to the dance and try to put his thoughts about the baby behind him.

When Monica and her gang were at the Wicker house, Anton was hurt Bob Wicker had lashed at him with the bowie knife he al-ways carried.

Anton had bad cut on the side of the face.

After a long dusty ride Monica found what she was looking for.

She pushed a bunch of branches out of the way that reveal a large boulder "Hey you lazy lot put your weight behind this boulder."

It was hard going at first but then it moved showing them a large cave.

Once they were inside Monica and the men moved the boulder back to cover the entrance.

Monica lit a torch and they walked though to a valley out the other side.

She had a house there that they did not know about till now.

Near the house was an old barn. They put their horses in it and an Indian came along to take care of them.

Before she let them to enter the house. Monica told them to take their boots off. They had to wash up as well using a basin of water and a towel on a stool at the door.

Once inside she disappeared in to one of the rooms where an Indian woman had a hot tub of water ready for her.

Another Indian brought the men a tray of coffee and some cigars. He never said anything just sat the tray down on a small table in front of the men.

After a long while Monica came out wearing a lovely dress with her hair put up high on her head with some nice combs in it.

All the men stood up when she walked into the room as mouth dropped to the ground.

"You guys can go with Crow he will show you where you can get cleaned up. While you are staying here in my house you will be gentlemen."

The men cleaned up and came out Monica had the table set for dinner.

When they all sat down she said "Now here is the thing the Indians here are more civilized than any other Indians and they are loyal to me. So don't get any ideas of trying to turn them against me."

The sheriff of Riverview was getting a lot of complaints about Monica and her gang.

He was a lazy sheriff who just wanted to sit around all day and do nothing but collect his pay check.

But this time the towns men held a meeting and sacked him. They found themself another man who.

Was younger and stronger he fear no one his name was Chad Wilkins.

Sheriff Wilkins did not waste any time he got a posse together and was out of town in no time.

Chad had an Indian friend named Two Feathers and he knew all the signs of tracking even if the trail was old and cold.

The dance at the Forte Ute the dance at Officer's club had just finished Kate and Jake were sitting on the porch of her Aunties home.

"Jake I am staying with My Aunty for a while I want to get my life back in order." "I hear what you are saying I'll send word when we have the gang behind bars so you can be at the trial if you want" Jake told her.

The next morning Jake and Albert said good-bye to all at the Forte and left.

The sheriff and posse searched along the river bed. Two Feathers found the ashes of a fire "Here Chad old fire."

"How long ago and how many?" Chad asked "Mmm three one woman two men about last night maybe" Two Feathers said.

They followed the trail and it took them straight to the Forte.

After talking to the colonel they found out that only Jake and Albert left.

Chad wanted to ask Kate some questions the Colonel took him to his quarters and said. "Kate this is the sheriff of Riverview he needs to talk to you."

Kate told the sheriff all she knew. Then Chad and the posse left as he wanted to catch up to Jake so they had to ride hard and fast.

This also meant travelling at night so they lit lanterns some of the posse did not like this "Sheriff this is dangerous we do not want to ride at night" Mac Travis said. Chad saw that Mac was right so he said.

"Ok you are right we will start at day break."

Jake and Albert were about one day ahead of the sheriff and getting closer to Monica's stronghold.

Not knowing just where she was they knew they had to find someone who knew the way and would talk.

Jake and Albert rode for a while and then to the Triple W ranch it was named that after it owners William Myers and his two sons Wayne and Walter.

They did not get to close to the house when a woman came out holding a double barrel shot gun. "That s far enough state your business" she called out.

"I am Jake North and this is Albert Jenkins we are trailing some bad outlaws have you had any trouble here lately." Jake asked

"I should say so get down and come on in"

She took them inside and said. "Hi I'm Heather Myers my husband and our two sons run this place."

William and his two sons had just come in from a long dusty round up of the cattle for market.

After shaking the dust off, they came inside.

"Hi I am William," he put out his hand to Jake.

Jake stood up and took his hand" We are here to see what you and your family know about some real bad outlaws that terrorizing people around here."

Wayne the elder son sat down next to his father and said "we had a bad run in with a woman and four men about three days ago"

"Yeah we run them off" Walter told them.

After they finished talking to the Myers Jake said "well it is time we were going thank you for all your help"

Walter out to get Jake and Albert's horse, He seemed to be taking longer than he should so his father called out "come on son these men need to be going" "dad you should see this" Walter called out.

Everyone went out to the corral "look I thought I hit one of their horses"

On the ground was a dying horse well all most dead. There was not much they could do except put the poor thing out of his misery.

"They must have taken the old horse we had here." Wayne said to his father "Well they won't get very far on that old plug it was past due for the glue factory."

Jake and Albert rode all day and then found a place to camp for the night.

They were finishing their last coffee before turning in for the night when Jake heard a noise in the bushes.

Albert stood up and called out "come out or you are dead where you stand." An Indian lady walked out looking very scared and pleaded "Please mister don't shoot me I will talk to you no shoot."

Albert said "Put your hands down and sit by the fire" "Now what are you doing out here and what is your name?"

Jake said "I know this lady she is called Batty. The other Indians think she is crazy." "I am not crazy I know a lot of things. You pay I will tell" she put her hand out.

Jake gave her coffee then they talked.

"Do you know where Monica and her bad men are hiding?" he asked. "Yes I will show you but first you give" she put her hand out again.

Albert had a beaded necklace he planned to take home with him.

He pulled it out and handed to the Batty. She smiled a toothless smile at him and said "yes now I will show you, I like you"

The next day they set out to find the outlaws it was hard going as they had to climb very high hills.

Soon they could ride no longer but had to get off their horses and walk.

"Jake I hope this lady is not leading us on a wild goose chase" Albert said

"Don't worry she know's what she is doing trust me" Jake assured him.

They came to a sheer mountain wall of rock.

"Oh great! A wall of rock now what?" Albert bellowed.

Batty pointed to a large boulder and said "English-man, you look here you push this boulder out of the way."

The sheriff was one day behind Jake and Albert when they were at the Myers ranch.

Chad wanted to catch up to Jake and knew he would have to ride hard and fast. "Men we have to ride hard and fast to catch up to Jake North."

"If anyone is not up to the task let me know now", Chad said then waited for a moment.

No one said anything he knew he had a crew that he could count on.

He and the men had a good night's rest. Then the next day they set out to catch up to Jake.

It was getting dark when Jake and Albert got to the mountain so they planned get an early start in the morning.

This gave Chad and his men time to catch up the next day.

Jake and Albert were having coffee when the sheriff rode up.

"Ah that smells good may we join you?" Jake looked around at the sound of a voice coming from behind them." First who are you and what do you want?" Jake asked.

"Straight to the point I like that I'm Chad Wilkins the sheriff of Riverview and this is my posse we are after Monica and her bunch."

"In that case you are more than welcome to join us" Jake said as he handed the sheriff a cup and told the others help yourselves.

Anton moaned about his face all day long and got every-ones nerves

"Anton your whining is getting on my nerves let me have a look at that scratch" Monica said then saw it had gotten bad.

She sent for the Indian doctor "I'm not letting no witch doctor look at it" Anton whined.

"You will do what I say or you will die from it is that what you want?"

CHAPTER 3

The chase

Anton had no choice so he let the Indian doctor have a look at it.

After Anton's face was attended to Monica said. "Men we have to move on we can't hang around here for too long."

Harold for one was glad he was board and looking some action.

As they were packing to leave a little girl came into Monica room.

She was a pretty little thing, very small with sparkling brown eyes and long jet black hair in a braid down her back.

"Mummy you go away again?" she asked. "My little angel mummy will come back soon, but you must be good Crow will take good care of you."

The little girl started to cry "You go away and Paula misses mummy" speaking in third person.

Harold came into the house and heard Monica talking to the little girl he thought—this was all they needed.

He knew they could use this against Monica as a weapon to get their own way.

Crows son, Little Crow, came to Monica and whispered *"You no go through the tunnel men are waiting on the other side."*

"Thank you Little Crow" Monica said.

Monica took her men through the cave a different way that came out the back of a waterfall.

"Why this way Monica it took us a lot longer than when we came in?" Sammy asked.

"Well my nosey friend if we went the short way we would run into the sheriff and company." "Oh just asking" Sammy responded.

Jake and the sheriff's men rolled the boulder back.

On the inside of the tunnel Jake found a torch that lit up the entire tunnel and gave them clear view of the way through.

They were surprised by what they saw when they came out. It was a small Indian village at least to the untrained eye. That is what the Indians wanted others to see

They headed for Monica's house but when they got there an Indian wearing a black suit greeted them.

"Hi I'm Jake North and this is my friend Albert these men behind me are the sheriff and his pose."

"We are looking for a lady and her gang of outlaws. Have you seen anyone like that around here?"

"No I am sorry can't say I have I am doctor Crow wont you come in and have some food and drink you look like you have come a long way."

Monica and her men headed south she heard about a plantation that needed cotton pickers.

"Oh Monica this looks like a good place to have some fun" Harold said.

"Yes but we must be careful when we start the fun there is always a lot of hands and servants around so leave it up to me."

The colonel was standing on the steps about to tell the hands what he wanted them to do. "Pardon me Colonel but could you use some more help? My men and I are in between jobs right now and we could do with some work" Monica told him.

"Oh my yes you are a godsend please go with the other picker and they will show you what to do and where you can bunk down and thank you."

The Colonel was a happy man he was going to get his cotton in on time or so he thought.

Jake Chad and Albert went inside while the posse and Two Feathers took the horses to the barn.

An Indian came out to them with some coffee and a plate of sandwiches for the men.

Two Feathers thought this would be a good time to ask him some questions.

He followed the other Indian to the barn.

"Hey what are you called?" Two Feathers asked.

"I am called Small Tree as I am smaller than others"

"I am called Two Feathers tell me who lives in big house."

"My boss the doctor and white lady" Small Tree said then was called away.

Jake Chad and Albert were ready to leave. They did not find anything to tell them that Monica and the gang were even there.

Two Feathers and the pose brought the horses out of the barn and they left the way they came in.

By this time it was getting late and they settled down for the night.

When Two Feather thought no one was listening, he told Chad about Small Tree saying a white lady was his boss.

Chad knew he meant Monica. The next day he told Jake that they did not come away empty-handed as they thought.

Now the problem was where did she go and how did she get out of the village without them seeing her.

"Jake how do you think she got away? We had the exit covered" Albert asked.

Jake thought about this for a while and could not come up with an answer.

Two Feathers said "I heard that there was an old way into the village"

"Oh where would that be" Chad asked.

Two feathers took them to the water fall where Monica came out and said "There you go in under the water."

"Under the water?" Albert did not understand until he saw Jake walk behind the waterfall "ah yes of course silly me."

In the tunnel Jake found a bandage that Anton threw away." look at this they did come this way and one is hurt."

Now their job was finding which way they went it did not take Two Feathers long to find the trail.

Two feathers said. "They go south fast, as he pointed in the direction they took."

"How far ahead would you say they are?" Chad asked.

"Hmm, about one day maybe a little more" "Hard to say" Two Feathers told him It was dusk so they decided to stop for the night and get an early start in the morning

Monica's men did not like doing manual labour and they complained all the time.

At the end of the day Monica and her men were shown a small cabin at the back of the others.

"You guys get your asses inside I want to talk to you" she said as she pushed them inside.

"Now, now Monica we know just what you are about so don't waste your breath" Sammy said.

"Well if you know what I was going to say how about giving me a break? You will get your fun later" she said not happy with their whining.

Monica knew she had to do something about these whiners. They have been coming a bit too much.

She thought maybe it is time to dump them and find another way of living.

Her daughter was on her mind all the time. She felt that she was not giving her the love and attention she wanted to.

Then Monica made up her mind this was going to be their last capper so she got the men together "Hey you guys lets have some fun" "ha that is more like it" Phillip said.

The five of them headed for the kitchen door the cook stop them before they got a foot inside.

"Stop right there. What do you want? You are not allowed in here." She said. She was a big woman, but it did not take much for Harold to push her out of the way.

"Out of the way woman we are looking for some fun."

The cook grabbed a large meat cleaver and got ready to swing it at the next one to walk thought the door.

That was Sammy, but Sammy was too fast for her. H e stepped past her, and turned took the meat cleaver of her, and it went straight in her back. She fell to the floor.

At this happened Susan Cutler came in to the kitchen, saw what happen she ran out.

"Get her Phillip she must not get away" Monica called out.

Susan ran right out the front door and down the road to her favourite hiding place.

With the noise they made it is a wonder it did not wake the whole house hole.

But the family was sleeping. The gang went from room to room taking all they could carry.

But what they did not count on was the butler seeing them. He woke the Colonel up.

Monica had had enough and took off long before the Colonel got to the house.

Because it was a hot night hotter than usual the men decided to sleep down near the lake.

Sammy saw the men come up the back steps "hey guys we have trouble let us get them."

Harold, Sammy and Aton hid behind the kitchen bench to surprise them as they came in. When the shooting started it got a bit out of hand and the gang knew it was time to make tactical retreat out of there.

Phillip caught up to Susan she was standing near the river where she went swimming.

Susan thought that Phillip had given up but she was wrong. He was watching her from behind some bushes as she undress and slip into the cool water. He liked what he seen her shapely body as she swam in the water.

When Susan out of the water and started to dress. Phillip could not control his urges he jumped out from behind the bushes and grabbed her held her down while he did what he wanted to do to her.

Susan screamed and screamed, then hit out at him, she kept on wiggling. She got away from him and ran as fast as she could half-dress.

When she got home the whole house was up and awake.

She got half way up the walk way and her father saw her, he grabbed his old army coat ran to her he wrapped her in his coat, and took her to her room, where her nanny to care of her.

The Colonel went into town to see the sheriff, but the only person he found in the office was the cleaner. Old Fred was sound asleep the Colonel poked him with his walking cane "wake up! Come on I need to know where the sheriff is."

After a few more pokes with the cane old Fred woke up and said. "Hey! stop that the sheriff is not here. He took a pose out a few days ago and has not come back yet."

When the Colonel heard this got even angrier he stormed out of the office.

He decided to take matters in to his own hand and find the ones that hurt his little girl.

Monica and her men knew where to meet up if they were separated.

There was an old abandoned mine they all knew about. Monica got there before the men got a fire going and had coffee on the boil.

She just sat back to relax when she heard a noise Monica stepped back with her gun out ready to shoot anyone who did not call out first.

Sammy called out "Monica you there?" "yeah you guys get your asses in here we need to talk."

The men walked into the mine sat down and grabbed a cup of coffee.

"-Well what is on your mind?" Harold asked "I'll tell you what is on my mine you are the pits. You could not wait till I gave the order. You just went head on in to the house. What a mess you made of it did you come away with anything at all."

Philip took of sip his coffee and he said "yes you will find two sacks on the horses out there see it was not a total loss." he boasted "you guys are lucky you did not end up dead" she argued.

While Monica and her men were hold up for a while Jake and the rest got closer and closer.

Two feathers put them on the right path and they found the trading post the gang all ways used

Chad had some of the pose to stay at the door and the others get around back to watch who leaves.

Three of them walked into the bar and ask the barman some questions but the barman was not forthcoming with answers. Albert grabbed the barman by the front of the shirt and drug him across the bar and said "The man asked you a question and we want an answer did see four men an Indian lady come in here in the last couple of days." "Um um yes sir they were here but they did not stay long." "Now that was not so hard was it?" Albert said as he let the barman go.

They went around the back to the others were waiting and told Chad that a young lad ran off into the barn nearby for a horse.

They knew just where he was going so they waited till he was out of sight and followed him.

The young lad led them straight to the old mine but Monica and the gang wre all ready gone.

Chad and the others went into the mine and learned that they had missed them by a few moments.

This puzzled them how did they know Two Feather told Chad "Lady can see in her mind when trouble is coming" "Oh you mean she has a sixth sense about these things" Chad asked. "Then this is how she is one step ahead all the time. We have no chance of catching them" Albert remarked.

"We will have out smart her and get one step in front of her" Jake told them.

"But how can we do this if we do not know which way she is going?" Albert asked

Monica and her men doubled back to the Trading Post where they sat around a table laughing.

While Monica and her men were having a good time they did not see the Colonel walk in.

The barman made a point of saying his name out loud. "Ah Colonel Cutler we don't see much of you these days"

When the gang heard this they lit out of there fast and the Colonel missed his chance.

Chad came up with an idea "We will set up a trap for her in town."

"Yeah what makes you think she is going to come to town"? Albert asked." If the stakes are higher enough she will come" Chad said.

Jake could see that Chad had something big in mind "I hope you are not thinking what I think you are thinking" Jake said.

This made Albert curious and he asked "What are you talking about?"

"Tell him Chad" Jake and said looked at Chad.

Chad nodded and said. "Ok the lady who leads the gang has a little girl. I am going to pick her and put her in the jail. When she comes for her then we will have her."

"You mean you are going to use her child as bait?" Albert asked

"Well yes I guess you can put it that way" Chad replied.

Albert was not happy with this but he thought it might the only way to catch the gang. He could only hope no harm came to the little girl.

When they got back in town Chad sent Two Feathers to get the girl and told him to take very good care of her

Two Feathers came into the sheriff's office limping with scratches on his face. He had the little girl wrapped in a blanket under his arm.

"Good god man, what happened to you?" Chad asked.

"Two Feathers put the little girl down on the chair in the office and said little she devil" then Two Feathers walked to the room at the back of the office.

Albert went to the little girl and started to un wrap her. She started screaming "I want my mummy" she screamed.

"don't scream we are not going to hurt you" Albert backed off.

It was Jakes turn to try to calm her "come on little one your mummy will be hear soon. Hear have drink water" he handed her a glass of water.

Paula took a shine to Jake and started to settle down "well Jake it looks like she trust you. So I would say you are it until her mother comes for her."

Monica and her men had no idea this happen. They found a cool river and set up camp to regroup and rest. They had just settled down when a rider came into their camp.

Harold stood up and said "that's far enough" Monica stepped in told Harold the rider was one of her men and asked.

"What do you want Grey Wolf?" "It is the little one she was taken to town by Two Feathers."

This made Monica very angry she walked around slapping her boot's with a riding crop she all ways carry then said. "I'm going to town to get my little girl I know who has her"

"But Monica it's a trap you better think about what you are doing" Anton told her "I don't care that is my little girl and I am not leaving her with them"

Monica open her pack and pulled out a Spanish lady's clothes "you don't think I am a complete fool do you?"

Monica set her men in and around the town in case of trouble they would have to shoot their way out.

Chad was working at his desk Jake and Albert sat at the other end of the office with their guns at the ready.

They did not have to wait long before Monica walked into the office.

"I am Marie Gomez I have come to take little Paula home to her mummy"

Monica kept her hand on her gun in the large pocket of long skirt.

Chad walked around the desk "What make you think we have the child here?"

"The Lopez family was told you had her here so they sent me to bring her home."

Just then Paula came running into the office from the back room and said "mummy I want my mummy."

She ran over to Monica and grabbed her skirt Monica picked up Paula and then pulled the gun out of her pocket.

She started to back towards the door but Jake put his gun in her back and said "You move and I will kill you" Jake meant every word he said.

Chad took Monica and Paula and put Monica in a cell He took Paula to the back room with Two Feathers.

Monica shouted at Chad "You won't get away with this. My men will get me out of here and you will be dead meat."

You know guys we are going to have a heap of trouble Albert reported.

Monica s men knew she was in trouble because she was taking too long.

Sammy slipped around to the back of the jail to the window where Monica was and whispered. "Psst hey Monica we'll get you out."

"Sammy is that you? Get my little girl first and take her home she is in the back room with an Indian. Take care"

Sammy went back to the men and told Anton to take care of the Indian in the Jail's back room

Two Feathers sat with his back to the door with Paula on his lap playing with the beads around his neck.

Anton came in very quietly and put his hand over Two Feather's mouth so he could not make a noise. Showing him the other hand where he held a large bowie knife.

Paula jumped off Two Feathers lap and ran out the door, then Anton pushed the knife into Two Feather's back he fell lifeless body to the floor. Sammy took Paula home to her nanny where she was safe.

They all heard Two Feather's fall to the floor and so did the others.

When they saw what happen Chad felt bad at seeing his friend lying there.

"I told you there would be trouble and it has started" Monica yelled from her cell."

"Shut up you bitch or you will not live long enough to for the district judge to get here" Chad yelled at her.

Albert went to get the under-taker but when he found out it was an Indian he said he could not do it.

Albert didn't understand this so he headed back to the office

"Hey Jake I asked the under-taker to come over and handle Two Feather's but he said he couldn't why?" Albert asked.

"Well my English friend, the Indians take care of their own they have their ways and we have ours" Jake replied

A little later the Indian chief came to the Sheriff's office.

Chad shook his hand and said" Sorry chief your son was a good friend to me"

"Not your fault it is that she devil you have in your jail she will die."

The Indian braves went to the back room and took their brother home

CHAPTER 4

Caught At Last

Monica sat in her cell and watched them take Two Feathers body out.

As they were leaving she could not help but to take a passing shot "yeah red-skin get that smell out of here" then she laughed loudly.

Chad heard what she said "shut your mouth half-breed" he shouted at her.

Monica sat down on her bunk with a smile on her face.

Then she heard a noise from the window of her cell.

It was Sammy who whispered *"hey boss we're ready to get you out to-night"*

About mid night, when all was quiet Sammy slipped in the back door that was never locked.

Chad and his men were out of the office.

Sammy grabbed the keys and let Monica out with no problem.

The next day they were a long way from town when it suddenly dawned on Monica that getting out of jail was too easy.

"My god it was a set up" she screamed.

"Well I have an idea how we can fix that" Harold commented.

They all sat around drinking coffee while Harold told them of his plan.

Chad Jake and Albert were sitting behind some trees not far away but not too close either.

"*Dam I would like to hear what they are saying*" Jake whispered to the others

"That would be too easy" Chad replied

While Chad and Jake were talking Albert slipped to try to get a little closer, but his foot slipped and pebbles started rolling down the hill-side.

Chad and Jake saw this happen and they got to him just in time to grab Albert by the shirt.

Anton saw Albert slip and told Monica

"Yes Anton we know" she said.

The gang ignored it as if they did not notice anything.

Late that night the gang made dummy sleeping area and slipped very quietly away.

Monica knew they could not go back to her place as that would be the first place they would look for her.

There was one place she could go and that was her old friend Allen Logan.

Allen owned a large plantation house with lovely gardens a porch that went all round the house.

When they got there Monica told her men to stay out of sight for a while she wanted to see her friend alone.

A butler greeted her at the door asking "yes how can I help you?" "I would like to see Mr Logan tell him it is an old friend"

"Oh you can come and wait in the drawing room" the butler said as he showed her to a large room where she could wait.

In a short time Allen came in and was surprised to see that his visitor was Monica "Monica it has been far too long how are you?"

"Allen my dear friend I am well but I need some help and you are the only person I can trust"

Monica started to weep Allen handed her a handkerchief "come come things cannot be all that bad. Tell me how can I help" Allen asked.

"Oh Allen I should not have come I have not seen you for a long time and now I am asking you for help it's not right I must go I'll be okay"

Allen went to Monica and put his strong arms around her and said "you know I will help in any way I can what is it that has you so upset?"

She knew she had sucked him in really well and could get him to do whatever she wanted.

Monica told Allen about how her farm was burned to the ground and that she and her hands were the ones who got out alive.

But she said they need some where to stay for a while. "Is that all that has you so upset."

"Of couse you can stay here with me and I can always use more hands they can stay in the bunk house now let's not have any more of those tears."

After talking a while Monica went to her men and said "Okay men we are in but you lot will have to stay in the bunk house. I do not want any whining. It will only be for a while oh yes no trouble from any of you."

It was late that night when Monica and her men were settled down.

The next morning Monica woke with breakfast on a tray.

The maid open the curtains and said "the master thought you may be hungry as you came in rather late last night"

"Oh yes thank you what is your name?"

"I am Josie the master said I was to be your maid so if you want anything all you have to do is ring that bell and I will come."

Jake was about to make coffee when Albert went to see if Monica and her gang were still there but there were not "hey guys the chickens have flown the coop," Albert called out.

"What on earth do you mean?" Chad asked.

"They have slipped out during the night they tricked us we thought they were asleep but they put logs in their beds and left."

This made Jake very angry "Damn we should have set a watch now we are back to square one"

Chad went to the gangs camp to look around it was a good thing that Two Feathers had taught him to read the signs.

He was able to pick up their trail easy enough. He told Jake he found it and after they ate they moved out.

Colonel Cutler was on the same trail as Jake and his men he knew the area well it was very close to his home.

Albert saw dust flying up behind them and said "Jake there are some boulder s up ahead we can get to them and wait to see just who it is following us."

The three men waited the rider got close. They came out with their guns drawn.

"who are you and why are you following us?" Jake asked.

The Colonel held his arms up and answered "I am colonel Cutler and I am not following you I live out this way"

Oh I'm sorry but we can't be too careful out here "Chad told him.

"Now maybe you would be good enough to tell me who you are and just what is your business out here?"

"we would be glad to but it's a long story and it's late maybe we should make camp and we'll tell you our story" Albert butted in.

The Colonel showed them good place to camp for the night.

After Jake finished telling Colonel Cutler what happened Colonel Cutler told them what had happen to his daughter.

"I would like to ride along with you guys and help get these bastards hell is too good for them."

Monica and her men were holed up at Logan's place but the men were getting restless.

These men were not the type of men to be cooped up for too long.

"This is no good we are men not chickens I say we go and find a town where we can have some fun" Phillip said.

"Yeah I'm with him" Harold responded. He was getting itchy feet but Sammy and Anton were not going to go against Monica's orders she was not one to cross.

When it got dark Harold and Phillip left and headed in to a small town nearby.

The next day Monica was up early and out for a walk she wanted to see the men just to make sure everything was as it should be.

When Monica got to the bunkhouse she saw Sammy and Anton but not Phillip or Harold.

"Where are the other two?" she asked Sammy and Anton did not know just what to tell her so they lied. "They went to the outhouse" Sammy said "What both of them together come on quit lying to me. Where are they this time it better good."

Anton kept looking at the door of the bunk house hoping they would walk in. "I'm waiting" Monica was getting impatient.

They knew they could not stall her any longer and would have to tell her.

Harold and Phillip were near the bunk house and heard Monica's voice one went to the back door and the other went in the front door. "You were looking for us?" Phillip asked

"Yes and where is Harold?" "I'm right behind you. A man cannot go to the outhouse round here or someone wants them or follows them. The next time you want to go Phillip I will make you hurry up" "keep calm It's that dam chilli we had last night."

Monica was not sure what was going on but she didn't care they were all there andthat is all she wanted.

After Monica left the bunkhouse the men playing cards

The foreman of the Logan place came and said "Men get your lazy asses in to the stables and start mucking them out"

"Yeah who said so and who the hell are to be giving us orders" Anton grumbled.

"First of all I am Mack the foreman around here if you have any complaints take them to your boss Monica"

The men did not argue any more just got to work they thought to take it up with Monica later.

Jake and the others were near to the Logan place when Albert asked "is there any other plantation around here Colonel?"

"Yes the Logan plantation is not far from my place it is a small place but Allen Logan makes a fine living out of it."

Allen was on his way to town when he ran into the Colonel and friends.

"Hey Allen I want you to meet some friends of mine. This is sheriff Chad Wilkins from Riverview and this is Albert Jenkins. He is from London hunting down an escaped murder."

Jake North is looking for the same gang that harmed my little girl.

Cutler told him "Oh yes Colonel I heard about that bad business I hope you get them I've got to go" Allen said as he rode off.

Allen rode back home as fast as he could he knew what Monica was afraid of she was running from the law.

But he could not turn her in as he found that he was in love with her.

He did not care what she had done he just wanted to save her from the law.

Allen took a short cut to his home that got him back in plenty of time.

When Allen got back he told Monica the law was hot on her heels.

"Monica I'm not going to turn you in I love you there I said it."

"Oh Allen you don't know what kind of women I am and what I've done yet you are willing to help me"

"Yes but we don't have much time I'll hide you in a small room at the top of the house. There will be no reason for them to go up there. Your men can take the old boat across the river to an old cabin. They will be safe there."

After Allen got the men across the river to safety he rode in-to town though the short cut.

Jake and the men arrived at the Logan place and were greeted by the butler. He told them master was not at home.

"Yes we know I am Sheriff Wilkins from Riverview and Mr Logan said it would be okay for us to have a look around.

"We are looking for a woman and four men. Have you seen any strangers around here?"

"No but you are welcome to search all you want"

Monica watched them though a small window at the top of the house.

The Colonel told Chad about the cabin across the river. "Maybe you should look in the cabin. There should be a small boat down there somewhere."

When Monica's men saw them heading down towards the river they left for a clump of boulder s not far from the cabin and were not found.

After Chad and the others had finished searching the Logan place the Colonel asked them to spend the night at his place.

Susan came down stairs just as Jake, Chad, and Albert came into the house Jake could not take his eyes off Susan to him she was the most beautiful lady he had ever seen.

"Susan I would like you to meet some friends of mine this Jake North, Chad Wilkins, and Albert Jenkins he has come here from England."

Monica thought if Allen loves me no matter what she I've done then this may be a good place to start a new life for me and my daughter.

She had to think long and hard about this. It was a big step to take.

The gang had got back to the bunkhouse and grumbling started.

"Guys I think Monica is getting to like this life I get the feeling she is going to dump us" Sammy said.

Harold looked at Anton and Phillip "Yeah I don't think she would do that__would she?" They asked.

That night they were restless and could not sleep thinking about what Monica might do. "Guys we need to sort this out now. I for one am not sitting around waiting for Monica to come in here and pick us off one by one"

"You think she would kill all of us one by one. Why?" Anton asked.

"Are you stupid or something any one of us can land her in jail and our self a long with her."

Harold said So we can get her first or just clear out. I'm for clearing out"

Phillip started to pack his saddlebag. "Then it is agreed we all just clear out. and go our separate ways. We hang on and we run scared We are jumping at shadows We don't know this is what Monica has in mind. I am staying until I hear it from her mouth"

Phillip stood firm.

After all the talk about leaving they all decided to stay and see what Monica was is going to do.

Allen and Monica sat down to dinner and Monica decided to tell Allen all about her little girl.

At the Colonels plantation they were about to sit down to dinner when Susan came down stairs wearing a lovely evening gown

Jake walked over to the stairs and held out his hand for her to take.

The Colonel had lent the men dinner cloths for the night.

So the men looked their best Thelma and Harry Cutler were very happy to see their daughter come down out of her room for the first time since the incident.

When dinner was over Jake ask Susan "Miss Susan would you show me your mother's lovely garden I have heard so much about it."

"I would be delighted" she said.

Albert and Chad sat in the drawing room with the Colonel and talked about the day and how it seemed to be getting harder and harder to catch Monica and her gang.

"She has so many people helping her how is this so?" Albert wanted to know.

"Well my English friend she gives a lot of money to a lot of people and helps them when they need it. So they help her in return" Harry said.

"Then this is a case of one hand washers the other" Chad commented.

"If we come up with a plan to dry up all that good-will, then maybe, just maybe, we can step in and take up the slack and get them to trust us and help us."

"Albert I think you may have something there good thinking Englishman" Harry said as he liked what he heard.

Monica's men were restless they had enough of waiting to see what she was going to do so they decided one of them would talk to Monica.

Sammy seemed to the right choice as he knew just what to say to her.

Sammy thought it might be better to use the servant's entrance but when he got around back he saw Monica kissing Allen it was not a goodbye kiss so he left.

Monica saw Sammy leave and knew it was time to talk to her men.

When Monica got the chance she went out to the bunk house to talk to the men. "Hi guys I think we need to talk"

"Yeah what about how you are playing kisses face with what-s his name" Sammy was in no mood to listen to what she had to say.

"Give her a chance to explain" Harold said as he wanted to know just where they stood.

"Guy's I'm thinking about changing my life for my daughters sake she is getting older and needs a stable life. But if Allen will not except my daughter then I guess it will be back to the old ways. Until I find what I want for my daughter I'll let you guys make up your own mind what you want to do."

The men were stumped they were not expecting this.

Well men I think we know where we stand I for one will be out of here we stay here and the law will catch up with us.

Allen won't protect us again Harold assured them.

The other men knew he was right and decided to go with him.

The next day the men packed up and left but what they did not know was that the Sheriffs men were watching the Logan house Chad had a feeling that Mr Logan was hiding the outlaws.

After awhile Harold spotted one of the Sheriff's men and alerted the others. One of the Sheriffs men rode tell Chad he was right.

Monica's men they knew they had move fast and hope they could get help at the Trading post.

When they got to the Trading Post old Joe was at the bar arranging the things on the shelves and did not see them come in.

"hey Joe it is me Sammy turn around you old coot" "Hey Sammy what have you and the others been up to it has been a long time. How is my good friend Monica?"

"Joe we need your help we have a tail and we have to get out of here" "Oh okay slip out the back there is a storage shed out there I'll head them off but tell Monica she owes me big time"

A few of the Sheriff's men came into the Trading post and asked Old Joe have you seen some stranger s come this way in the last few minutes

"Um no I have not any of you others seen anyone" he asked his other customers.

No they all said.

They were not going to say they did that would be biting the hand that feeds them.

In the shed Sammy told the others that they better get out of there fast they headed for the water fall and the tunnel to Monica's home.

When they reached Monica's home they found Monica there.

Anton was the first though the door "hey Monica you're here we thought you were staying with Allen"

"I know Anton I was but we had a miss understanding this nothing for you and the men to worry about. I'm back and we can get back to things as usual."

While Monica and Anton were talking the rest of the men came in they were just as surprised to see Monica as Anton was.

"Ah this is good we are all back together" Phillip announced

Jake and the other men rode to the Trading post to meet up with the other men.

When they caught up Chad asked "well men what did you find out? Where are the outlaws now?"

"Sorry boss we lost them the bartender said he had not seen any strangers all day."

"Darn the same old thing. They are protecting the outlaws. Jake I've decided to go back to town. There is not much we can do now."

"That's right you give up okay, Fine you go back with your tail between your legs Albert and I will carry on." Jake said very angry at Chad s decision.

Albert knew that Chad had not given up He wanted to make a new plan and look at it from a different angle.

"I'm sorry Jake I'm with Chad we are not giving up as you put it. We just want to look at this from a different angle. Come back with us Jake and we can work something out. All we are doing now is running around in dam circles. Every time we get close someone helps them out and we miss out" Albert said. He hoped that Jake would see that he was right and go back with them.

"I'll stay here I want to look about some more. If I'm not back in town in three day's come looking for me. Okay guy's" Jake asked them.

As Albert and Chad rode off in one direction and Jake went the other Albert said. "Chad do you think Jake will be all right out here?" "Hell yes he knows this country well"

Back at town Chad and Albert settled down in Chad's office to try to find away to stop Monica and her men.

CHAPTER 5

Trap's

Monica had all the entrances to the valley where she lives booby trapped.

Only the people who lived there knew how to get past the traps.

Jake went thought the tunnel behind the water-fall. He was near was the other end but did not see the trip wire at the entrance of the tunnel in to the valley.

When he tripped the wire a heavy net came down him and his horse.

"What the hell what is this?" he yelled.

Jake made so much racket that guards heard him and came to look One big guard stood there laughing "Oh my god now look at the fish we caught Monica will want to see this one"

He knew just who it was they had in their net.

They took Jake to the barn tied him up and went to get Monica.

When Monica saw just who they caught she could not stop herself from laughing "Ha, ha, ha, will all my dreams come true" Monica walked up to Jake and lightly tapped him on the face with her riding crop.

Monica was having so much fun when she remembered that Chad and Albert were still out there somewhere. "Now Jake old friend do you think you could tell me where your friends are?" She knew he would not tell the truth but she had to try.

"Go to hell I will tell you nothing" Jake said

"Oh nice you first" Monica walked away slapping her boot with the riding crop.

Chad and Albert had not come up with answer to a way of getting things turned around.

They had to work out just who was been helping Monica and get them on their side.

Albert had an idea "Maybe we could offer them protection and help them any-way we can"

"Yes Albert that might work. We can try but first we have to find Jake and see if he thinks it will work."

When Monica entered the house she heard the men talking in the kitchen and asked

"What are you planning now?"

Sammy turned and said "We need some action we are bored"

"Oh you will get some action soon enough, but not the kind you are thinking of."

"What is going to happen Monica?" Harold wanted to know.

When Monica had told them all about what just happen this made they got excited.

The men went out to the barn and saw Jake hanging by his arms from the beams barn they stood there and laugh.

Albert and Chad went to the Trading Post. They thought rather than wait to see Jake they would try it out on old Joe. Old Joe told them that it sound al-right but it was up to the other people they had to have a meeting.

It was just on dark when Chad and Albert got to the waterfall they thought Jake might have come this way so they set up camp.

The next morning they woke to guns in their faces.

"Who the hell are you and what do you want?" Chad asked.

"We are friends of Old Joe he tells us you want to make a deal." "Yes but this is no way of doing it. Put your guns away and we can talk."

They started a fire put coffee on to boil and Chad told them their plan.

It was a good plan and the men were happy with it.

"This is a good plan and We'll tell the other that it is. You have a deal."

After the hand shaking Chad and Albert left for the tunnel behind the water fall.

They walked carefully though the tunnel. When they had come to the end they stopped and looked around from inside the tunnel.

Chad was about to move on when Albert grabbed him and stopped him from going any further

"Why did you stop me? It is all clear"

"Yeah look down at your feet__ a trip wire."

Chad moved back and saw the wire. It led to a large net in the roof of the tunnel. "Yeah a booby trap that figures. They are not taking any chances of someone coming in uninvited."

After that Chad and Albert were more careful where they stepped and kept a close eye out for an ambush.

Jake was in a lot of pain but was not going to let them know although at one stage he asked for water.

Anton was on guard and said "You want water do you"? He walked over to Jake with a dipper of water and tormented him with it.

"Please I'm dry" Jake begged.

Then Anton tossed the dipper of water in Jake's face.

While he was jumping around having fun he failed to see Chad and Albert.

They came up behind Anton and hit his head with a gun butt.

Anton went down for the count, out like a light. They got Jake down quickly but he was so weak he could stand up.

They swang Jake over his saddle and lead his horse out to where they had left their horses.

They were al-most back at the tunnel when bullets were flew pass their heads. "Come on Albert we have to make a run for it" Chad yelled

They slapped Jakes horse hard on the rump and it took off in the direction of the tunnel

They made to the tunnel and right though to the water-fall when Chad saw that Albert was hit in the shoulder.

"Bloody hell now I have two men down"

Monica's men failed to give chase. That gave Chad time to find a place to get a fire started and do what he could for Albert.

As for Jake it was a matter of rest and time and he would be al-right.

Monica was not happy that Anton was so stupid he let someone sneak up behind him.

She went on and on about "Yeah Monica I know and you won't let me forget it any time soon"

"You're dam right about that you better get out of my sight for now"

Anton went out slamming doors, thumping walls,-jumped on his horse and rode off.

He rode to the nearest place where he could get a drink and that was the Trading Post.

Old Joe gave him a bottle and a glass and he sat at a table in the corner.

Anton was in no mood to be around other people or talk to anyone.

Old Joe decided to waited until Anton drank at less half the bottle of whiskey then he would ask him some questions.

Chad knew that the bullet in Albert's shoulder had to come out and he had to do it.

Albert had passed out from the pain so Chad had to work fast he heated up his knife he had and dug the bullet out.

With the bullet out and the wound bandaged Chad fixed coffee then sat back and rested.

After a while Jake sat up and found that he could walk. He had the feeling back in his legs again.

"I see you are all right now, that's good Jake, will you check on Albert?" Chad asked.

Just as Jake bent over Albert to see if he had come too Albert moaned. "My shoulder the pain oh . . . dam it dose hurt."

"It should hurt pal you had a bullet dug out of it if you take it easy for a few days you'll be al-right" Jake warned him. "I'm sorry but we must move on. It's dangerous out here Monica might decide to send someone out to see if we are still around."

Monica did not like the way Anton lit out, so she sent Sammy to track him down and bring him back.

By the time Sammy found Anton he was good and drunk and had al-ready spilled his guts to old Joe and then passed out on the table.

"Anton tell me you did not say anything you should not have?" Sammy pushed Anton but all Anton did was grunt. Sammy pushed him again harder this time.

Anton said "Do that again and you are a dead man" he screamed

"Anton it is me Sammy come on we're leaving Wake up you Mexican bastard" then Sammy pushed again.

"Okay okay I'm up but I think I need help to get on my horse, ha, ha, ha," Anton said not able to walk.

Sammy helped him on to his horse.

When they got Anton back Sammy dumped Anton in the bunk-house to sleep it off.

Sammy did not like doing this kind of dirty work for Monica he went to her and said "Monica we need to talk"

"Yeah about what?" wait first lets should get the others in on this. They have a right to hear this and to have their say "Okay Sammy I'll have everyone to dinner to-night and then we can talk"

Monica had a fair idea what it was all about and was one step ahead of Sammy.

After dinner they sat and talked Sammy was the first "Monica I think Anton has to go we cannot trust him anymore. I don't know how much he told old Joe but my sense is that Old Joe has gone over to the other side."

Monica asked the others what have they saw or heard Anton say "I have heard that some people are tired of waiting for your help they are going elsewhere."

Phillip said "I've I heard the same but more is what I saw last evening."

"Well spit it out just what did you see" Monica wanted to know all they had to tell her.

"Monica Anton has been meeting a Mexican Lady just about every night and they are having very long talks."

Monica walked up and down the room thinking *"have I lost my touch, am I losing my grip"* She said let me think on this and I'll let all of you know when I have make up my mind what I am going to do about Anton.

Chad and Jake got Albert back to town and had the doctor take a look at him.

When Chad got back to the Old Joe was waiting for him.

"Sheriff we need to talk I have a lot to tell you" Old Joe said as he sat down. He started to tell Chad what he found out from Anton then hesitated. "But before I tell you any more you said you would help us is that still on?"

"Yes Joe I will in any way I can" Chad assured him.

"Okay then this is what I got from Anton" they sat and talked for a long time Chad was not surprised that Monica would try something like this all her avenues were drying up.

She could not help the people when she was on the run.

Old Joe left the Sheriff's office and Chad went to check on Albert and tell Jake what he had found out. "Hi Jake how is Albert?"

"The doc said he will be al-right with some rest and a bit of attention from Kate"

"Hey is Kate here? That will make Albert happy I know those two had something going back at the forte" Chad was glad to see Kate arrive.

The next day at the Trading Post a wagon full of supplies left with no note to say where it came from but Old Joe knew.

He had the wagon unloaded and sent the driver went back to town.

Anton was in the bunkhouse nursing a bad hangover that was taking two days to get over.

He knew he was running out of time and Monica would put out the order out to deal with him soon.

He got his things together and saddled his horse, When it got dark he would leave but he was gone.

The next day Monica sent the other men out to deal with Anton.

"Oh crap. Now Monica will want us to go and find him" Sammy said.

They did not like this as they wanted to get back to doing what they wanted.

Now it was an all out search for Anton the first place they looked was the trading Post. "Old Joe have you seen Anton?" Phillip asked

Old Joe shook his head and said. "No" He did not want to have much to do with them. but he wanted to know why they were hunting down Anton. He thought he knew, but needed to know if he was right, so he asked "Hey guys what has you in such spin about finding Anton?"

"He has to be found he let the side down badly and we have to deal with him."

The gang decided to go in the other direction and pretty soon they picked up his trail.

He left a trail of destruction everywhere he went. They came up to farm where they found a young woman laying in a bed with a sheet over her.

The young woman looked as if she had no cloths on her and son was sitting on a chair next to the bed.

Sammy went to the boy and said "Son I think you should come out to the kitchen with me I need to talk to you

"Sammy put his hand out to the boy to show he was friendly."

At first he did not want to leave his mother but with a little coaching the boy went with him.

Phillip sat on the bed and tried to talk to the woman and ask her if they could do anything for her.

She said "no just find the dirty Mexican who raped me and killed my father and stole all of our life savings"

"Where is your father's body ma'am we will bury him for you" Harold told her.

Harold found the body out in the barn he dug a grave for him and they all stood there for a while so the boy could say good bye to his grandfather.

When they finished at the farm and knew that had done all that they could they headed back on their way looking for Anton.

It did not take long before word got around town about what had happen at the Hensley Farm.

The ladies of the town rallied around and went out to do whatever they could for Pam and her boy.

Chad and Jake got a posse together and rode out to find Anton hoping they might get the rest of the gang as well.

But the gang was a long way ahead of Chad and the posse.

Sammy found some hot ashes and they knew that Anton was not far away.

It was not long before they caught up with Anton sleeping in someone s barn. He did not hear Sammy and the others come in.

"Wake up you bastard you're coming back with us" Phillip said as he kicked him in the ass.

Anton jumped to his feet quickly and said. "Go to hell I'm not coming back with I'm a dead man if I do" Anton back up and drew his gun.

Harold walked in front of Anton and said "Put that gun down or you will be a dead man where you stand. Anton you don't know that this is what Monica has in mind for you come back and find out" Harold lied thought his teeth just to get Anton to put the gun down so they could grab him.

Jake and Chad picked up Anton's trail quickly and made up good time.

One of the posse men told Chad of an old farm not far from them and that there was an old barn still standing.

As soon as they got close to the barn Chad ordered the men to surround the barn.

Jake and Chad went very carefully to the door of the barn listened for a while but could not hear anything.

With their guns drawn they entered the barn. They found was Anton shot though the heart it looked like he must have put up a fight, but he lay face down in the dirt. Chad told the men to tie Anton's body to his horse to take him back to town for burial.

"Damn I was hoping to get all of them. Well now at least there one less to worry about" Jake said with anger.

When the men got back to the valley without Anton Monica knew what happen they did not have to say anything." Al-right maybe it is for the best.

Now we can get on with my new plan" she said with a smile on her face.

The men knew that Monica was back to herself let the game begin.

Jake wondered why Chad had the body taken back to town it was not just for a burial.

"Chad why are have Anton's body taken back to town don't tell me it is to give him a proper burial"

"You my friend are very smart no I want to see if anything on him can could be useful"

"Ah you also a smart man I like your way of thinking" Jake was happy about this.

But their joy was short lived there was nothing on Anton except a poor photo of a woman. It was very hard to see just who it was. But when Jake turned it over it had some writing on it in Spanish.

Jake took the photo to a lady at the cantina in town he wanted to know what it said. "Si senor this is a photo of a man's wife I know this lady."

"Thank you do you know where I can find her"

"Si senor she works as a cleaner for the hotel here in town"

Jake could not believe his luck he thank her and went back to the jail.

Jake told Chad that he found out who the lady in the photo is

"Yeah who is she?" "She is Anton's wife I am going to see her to tell her that husband's dead"

CHAPTER 6

New Cappers

Monica and her gang were on their way to rob a train this was a new capper for her and her men.

They put a large pile of logs across the railroad track to stop the train.

When the engineer on the train saw the logs on the tracks he had to stop in a hurry."

Mac, get some men to help us move those logs of the track" Ben called.

While they were removing the logs Monica and her men boarded the train and started robbing the passengers when Phillip saw a beautiful young blond girl wearing a dress that showed a lot of her breast and he could not take his eyes off her.

Monica saw that Phillip was eyeing her so she called out. "Okay if you want her so bad take her but we have to go"

Phillip grabbed her by the hair and said "Come on you are coming with me" The girl screamed but he would not let her go.

As the last log was moved from the tracks the gang jumped off the train and rode off for.

By this time most the passengers were off the train screaming at Ben that they were robbed and that a young girl was taken against her will.

"Okay get back on the train when we get into Riverview I'll make a report and the railway will pay compensation."

When the train pulled into the Riverview station Ben headed straight for the station master to send a message to the head of the railway.

Phillip was having fun with the girl. He striped her dress off.

She was a shy little thing who stood in her underwear and crying.

Phillip could not stand was a women crying.

He walked around the room wondering what do to stop her crying.

It was getting on the other's nerves to as well.

"Phillip shut that bitch up or I'll her shut up permanently" Sammy called out.

Phillip slapped the girl hard across her face.

She screamed out loud and this made the others madder so Phillip took her outside

He took her to an Indian chief he knew and said "Here chief she's a gift for you and your braves" He threw her on the ground.

"How is called?"

"I don't know, I did not ask, Call her what you want" Phillip said glad to get rid of her.

Monica saw Phillip come back from the Indian's camp and asked "What did you do with that girl?"

"I gave her to the chief as a gift. He will take good care of her" Phillip just walked away laughing.

Jake went to see Anton's wife then found out that al-ready knew.

That meant that someone came in to town, told her and left without been noticed.

"Chad we have a spy in town, Someone is coming and going as he or she pleases."

"This person knows every move we make I think we better find out just how it is" Jake said very serious about this.

"Al-right Jake but what makes you think we have a spy?"

Jake explained "when I went to see Anton's wife she all ready knew about her Anton and didn't won't to talk to me."

Chad had to agree there was a spy so the next step was to set a trap for whoever it is.

They sent out the word that Anton's wife needed help.

Jake was sure the help would come from somewhere inside Monica's camp. He also thought he knew who was relaying the messages.

Jake and Chad sat that night waiting. Finally they saw someone in the shadow down the alley near the hotel's back door.

They went quietly down the keeping out of sight.

They heard someone calling Anton's wife, "Maria, Maria I have come what is it you need help with"? the voice said. It did not sound like anyone they knew.

A light came on in the back room of the hotel "Senor I did not send any message to you I'm sorry you must leave quickly this is a trap."

"Yes it is" they said as both men came out and grabbed the spy.

They took the spy back to the jail so they could see who they were dealing with.

When they took the cape off the spy's head they were shocked to see it was an Indian lady.

"Who is helping you get messages" Jake asked her.

"There are a lot of people some here in town some at Trading Post."

This fit what Jake thought "So I know one at the Trading Post must be old Joe yes" "I say no more or I will die you let me go now yes"

"You tell us who in town is helping and you can go" Chad said. He had to know who the other helper in town was.

Jake had a fair idea who it was "If I guess who it is all you will have to do is nod your head, is it Miss Gaby?"

The Indian lady nodded her head yes.

After she answered all of their questions they let her go.

They knew just where she would go straight to Old Joe.

Jake and Chad did not know quite what to make of this as they both thought Anton took information back to Monica.

But they were wrong it's someone else in Monica's camp and they were working against her.

At the Trading Post the Indian Lady stopped of to see Old Joe "She told him we have heap big trouble. Men at jail caught me and made me tell all"

Old Joe took the lady out back and said "You go home I will handle this" Old Joe knew he had to talk with Chad and Jake.

While all of this was going on Albert was getting better seeing more and more of Kate.

Albert did not forget why he was there he had to get back to work soon and had to tell Kate.

When Old Joe got to jail he was not alone. He brought a girl with him.

He walked into the jail Chad and Jake were talking about seeing him.

"There you two idiots are what makes you think we are passing information to that bitch Monica?" Old Joe said standing his ground.

Jake looked up from a paper he was holding and asked "Joe what brings you here?"

"First I want you to meet someone," he took girl by the arm led her close to the desk and then took the old army coat off her. She was wearing a ripped dirty blood stained dress her hair was a mess. "I don't know this girl's name all I can get out of her is train and Indian and sometimes she screams don't Joe put the coat back on her."

As they were talking Albert walked in with Kate and the girl ran off to sit in a corner.

"This is all she will do she is so scared of people" Joe pointed out.

Kate took a closer look at the woman she thought she knew her.

"Kate do you know this girl?" Albert asked "So Joe is this what your visit is all about"

"No Chad I want to tell you and your people to back off we do not run messages to that bitch Monica; we help people that harmed. We let her think she has the upper hand so we can come and go as we want. We will get that bitch and her animals so back off all you are doing is mudding the waters."

"Sorry Joe but I can't let you take the law into your own hands but we will keep your secret."

With that Joe left of the office mumbling idiots the lot of them.

Kate took a close look at the girl and let out an all mighty scream "Molly is that you?" Kate put her arms out to the girl "Molly my baby sister. The girl ran to Kate and sobbed" "Katie you found me" she said.

Kate left to take care of her sister.

"Now guys where are we at the moment? I need to get back to work and do what I was sent here to do" Albert said anxious to get started again.

"Slow down there pal has the doc said you can go back to work" Jake asked.

"I don't give a fig what the doc says it is what I say that counts and I say I feel good enough to get out there and find that bastard I'm looking for."

A buggy pulled up at Monica's house and a well dressed man got out.

Monica greeted him at the door "ah how nice to see you again Markus"

She took him into the study where they would not be disturbed.

While they were talking the men came in and asked who was in there.

"Does anyone know who she is talking to" Sammy asked.

There was no answer no one knew just what was going on.

To avoid the others, seeing Markus Monica let him out the patio doors.

When Monica came into the living room where the men were, they wanted to know who he was.

That man was my connection to the coming and going in town. He told me that a big shipment of money was leaving on the stage coach in the morning, so I need you guys to be ready. Oh yes Phillip do not grab any more girls. The chief is still angry about losing the last one. I think we have a traitor in camp that is helping the sheriff. We need to seek this traitor out.

The next day Monica and her men were out on the road waiting for the coach.

As soon as the coach came around a bend in the road the guard saw the gang waiting for them.

The guard started shooting his rifle and the gang fired back the driver tried to turn the coach around but he was shot.

Phillip came in close grabbed the rains and stop the coach.

Harold shot the guard before he could get another round off Sammy open one coach door Monica opened the other and ordered everyone to get out.

The gang took the strong box and robbed the passengers.

To prevent the passenger's from sending the law after them they took the horses as well.

The coach was about three miles out of town a long walk back.

There was an elderly couple in the group so it was slow going they had to stop every so often to let them rest and drink some water.

They were thankful the gang did not take the water.

By the time they got back to town they were carrying the old lady and two others were helping old man.

Markus in the bank saw them though the bank window and ducked further inside.

Chad came out to the group and asked "What happened here?"

They told him the stagecoach was held up, robbed and added "And they took all of our money and jewellery."

Jake could easily guess who was at the bottom of this. "Well Chad she has changed tactics she has taken to robbing trains and stagecoaches. What will she try next?" Albert found it hard to understanding this woman she was out of his league.

"When you think you have her pinned down she rises up and goes in another direction" Jake observed.

Kate came into the office with a piece of paper in her hand" My sister is a good artist she drew a picture of the man who attacked her" Kate showed it Albert

"Kate dear we know just who we are after" Albert said as he handed it to Chad and Jake.

Both men picked up on the Kate dear

"Oh what do we hear Kate dear" Chad laughed.

"Well we were going to tell all of you later but I suppose now is as good as any Kate and I are engaged to be married.

Albert said standing with his arm around Kate.

Chad and Jake were both happy about the news "So Albert when is the big day?" Jake inquired.

"Not until we wrap up this case."

Monica had a meeting with her men after the robbery.

"Men we have done very well with this haul but we need give some of it to our people who are in need. We also have to go in a different direction next time"

Phillip was not happy with the way things were going. They take all the risks and then she gives some of it away. She never did this before. "What are you up to Monica we never give any to these people before?" Phillip asked.

"Are you that dumb? I have al-ways given a little to the people who need it. We must keep them on our side. I gave it to out of my cut but now I have to ask you to help Things are getting harder and harder. So quit your bellyaching and ante up" Monica said in no mood to argue.

The men did not like this much and did a lot of grumbling.

The men stayed in the bunk house they did not want to stay in the big house so they could talk freely.

Monica went to see Old Joe and gave him some of what they took. But she found that she did not feel as welcome as she once was. "Joe what is going on here I have some good help for you why am I not welcome" and asked "Joe what is going on here? I have help for you. Why am I not welcome anymore?"

Old Joe told her what was going on and that he did not like it. He knew just what she would do. "Monica we do not need your help any more. You better not come here There will not be any more help for you and your men" Old Joe said and walked away.

As Old Joe expected she did not take the news very well. She started shooting up the Trading Post. Then said "you will regret this, mark my words." Then she left.

When Monica got back the men were gone this made her angrier than she ever before

A few days later the men came back Monica was waiting for them and asked "Where the hell have you bastards been for the last few days?"

Sammy said "You know sometimes men have to let off steam so we went up north to have some fun."

Monica thought that over seemed to be satisfied and said "Well come inside we need to talk."

She told them about old Joe and made plans to get even with him.

Old Joe knew Monica did not make idle threats so he made plans to move before Monica could do anything to him and his family.

That night after Old Joe and his family went to bed. Monica and her men rode up and started a fire in the storage shed out the back.

The fire quickly spread to the main building and Old Joe found himself and his family trapped.

He planned to make the big move the next day as he thought he had time.

Old Joe knew he had to get his family out somehow As luck would have it a rider came by looking for a place to stay the night When he saw the fire he stopped and helped Old Joe with his family get out of the fire.

"Thank you stranger. You have just saved me and my family from certain death I'm in debt to you."

Now they all needed somewhere to stay "Come with us. I know some people not far from here and who will help us" Old Joe said as held his hand out to shake the stranger's hand. Then he saw that he only had one hand

Joe was curious about this man and how he lost his arm.

Monica and her men watched the fire from behind nearby trees. They were disappointed when the stranger helped Old Joe "I want to know who that man who help that rat out of the fire is. I think I've crossed his path before you guys get out there and find out. And don't come back until you do." Monica said seeing red anyone who got in her way was in got trouble.

CHAPTER 7

Trapped

William Carter the stranger who helped left before anyone got up. He had to a job to do. Old

Joe wanted to talk to the man who saved his family's life but he was gone.

He asked around for anyone who saw him but no one had seen him before.

Monica's men were hot on William's trail. They followed him along the river

They wanted make sure they did not lose him.

When it got dark William stopped and made camp. He knew someone was following him so he put a big log next to the fire and sat his hat on it.

Monica's three idiots did not remember this was a trick they had used.

William found nearby bushes and waited. He knew they would fall for the trick.

Sure enough they snuck in and tried to put a sack over the hat. William came up behind and pulled his gun behind them and said. "Well what do I have here Monica s three rats now tell me what you want from me?"

"Monica sent us to bring you back to her. She wanted to talk to you" Sammy said with a nervous tone to his voice.

"You don't think I am going to fall for that do you?"

"No tricks she just wants to talk to you" Harold said getting un easy with the gun at his back.

"Please mister, just come back with us our lives won't be worth living if you don't" Phillip begged.

"Oh I'll be seeing Monica soon enough. But I'm not going back with you."

Now unbuckle your gun belts and drop them behind you then.

Take your boots off and put them behind you "Come on it is bad enough you are taking our guns but our boots" Phillip whined.

William did not stop there he made them take all their clothes off. The only thing he left with was their long johns.

He took their belongings and rode off leaving them standing there wondering what to do.

They were still standing there when a carriage with four women came along. They were looking for a place to spend the night.

These were not ordinary ladies, they were different.

When they saw the three men standing in their under wear they took pity on them and gave them some old clothes they had collected for the poor.

"Here you are. You look like you could use these you poor things. Were you robbed?" "My name is Hope these are my sisters Faith and Charity and the older lady is our mother Mrs Beth Cooper."

The men did not know quite what to make of theses ladies so they made them as comfortable as they could.

The next morning the men were gone before the women woke up.

Old Joe came into town for help from Jake and Chad.

"Sheriff you have to do something about that Monica and her band of bastards, They torched my place two nights ago and if it wasn't for a stranger who came by we would all be dead. Now we need to somewhere to live and start the Trading post again."

Jake sat Old Joe down gave him some coffee and said "Joe we will help you find another place now can you tell us about the fire? We know who ordered it but what we don't is why"

While Jake talking to Old Joe Chad had went out to round up some men for posse.

He did not want just anyone, He asking for single men who did not mind staying out on the trail for as long as it took to get this business of Monica and her outlaws finished one way or the other.

Albert heard that Chad was rounding up a posse and he wanted in on it too.

Kate also had a stake in this so the both of them went to talk to Chad.

William knew how to get in to Monica's camp without been seen or caught in any trap she had installed since the last time he was there. His thoughts about the last time he was there brought back lot of memories all bad.

He went thought the tunnel and into the camp without problem. Now he had to get to his mother's home without being seen.

He hid in the tall trees near the tunnel until dark and then made his move.

Monica's men returned got back to camp and none of them had the guts to tell Monica how they failed.

After a good night sleep Sammy woke and said" Ok you cowards we all go to Monica and tell her" "Tell Monica what? How you three idiots failed me" she screamed.

There was no way of getting out of this one so they just had to take whatever she dished out.

Chad was in the front of the jail giving the poses their instructions.

Kate walked up to Chad and said. "We need to have a talk inside" Kate and Albert went inside the jail.

Jake was al-ready there and said "Hi you two come to see us off?"

"No, we came to go with you" Albert said "Well no we will not be need you this time" Chad said coming in behind them.

"May I remind you Chad that I have a prisoner to catch and take back to England" Albert responded standing fast on this one.

"Okay you can come but as for you Kate"

"I go too I will not take no for an answer you know I am very good with a gun and I think you need me" Kate interrupted.

"Early the next morning they started leave but were stopped by Old Joe" This is where I draw the line Joe you are too old to come thank you all the same

"Chad said putting his hand up in a stop sign."

That's good because I'm not asking to come with you I had to tell you something before you go. There is a man out there name William Carter. You might look him up he will be a big help to you when you get to Monica's camp"

"Yeah how will I know this man" "Easy he only has one hand."

William got into his mother's home without trouble. His mother was pleased to see her son again "Son you should not have come. You know what they did to your poor father and you."

She was worried they would do the same or worse.

William put his arm around his mother "Mon I am ready for them this time she only has three idiots with her now and I can handle them no worries."

An Indian came to Monica and whispered to her "*he is back at his mother's*"

"Thank you Jimmy you are a good boy tell cookie to give something out of the special jar."

Monica headed straight for Mrs Carter's house. Luckily William saw her coming he ducked out the back.

"Ethel I was told your son came back I thought I told him he was a dead man if he came back" Monica said.

This gave William time to get around to the front door.

He put his gun to Monica's head and said "Come in Monica don't be a stranger please come in" he pushed her in to the front room and made her sit down. "Get a rope mom." "You are not going to tie her up are you son?" "Yes that's not as bad as what she did to me, but that is about to change" William answered not forgetting what happened to his father and him.

Chad and his men were not far from the water fall when Jake said "we should stop here and get a fresh start in the morning"

"Yes, good idea We'll have a lot to face then" Albert agreed.

Phillip was pacing up and down in the bunk house.

"Hey stupid what has got you tied up in knots?" Harold wanted to know.

"Yeah all that up and down is getting on my nerves" Sammy put his two cents worth.

"Well I am sick and tired of jumping every time that bitch comes slapping her boot with that riding crop. I would like to shove that thing down her throat."

"yeah I know just what you mean having a woman order us around like sheep" Sammy said getting angry.

"Well lads what do you think we should do about it?" Harold asked.

The men did not want stay.

They agreed to have a night on the town and talk to Monica later they owed her that much.

William and his mother went to bed that night leaving Monica tied up on a chair.

"Son do you think it is a good idea to leave her sitting there all night?" Ethel asked.

"Yes Mom I do now don't worry get some sleep". William answered put his arm around her shoulders.

When Monica thought everyone was a sleep she tried to free herself but the rope was tied too tight.

The more she struggled the tighter the ropes got and one was cutting into her wrist.

She knew what William had in mind, She wondered if the hot coals were next.

The next day the men were back from their romp in town they left one woman dead raped repeatedly by all of them, She had a heart attack and died.

They went over to Monica's house they thought they had better get it over with.

When they got there her servant told them that she had not been home since yesterday after-noon.

This got the men thinking It was not like her to stay away unless she was on a job or out having fun.

"This is strange let's give her a bit of time and see if she turns up on her own" Sammy waited for a reply.

"And if she does not come back in a while do go looking for her Phillip wanted to know."

Ah she might be drowning her sorrows and lost track of time. She'll turn up sooner or later" Harold was sure of this.

Chad and the men entered the tunnel and walked slow towards the end watching for traps.

As they got to the end Jake told them to look down at the ground for thin wire.

"It will be stretched from one rock to the other if you trip it a large net will come down on you."

Jake found the wire pointed it out to everyone and said. "See what I mean? When we get out I'll trip it. That is not the only thing that happens. Soyou had better get out of sight and cover your ears"

"Why Jake what else will happen" Albert wanted to know.

"Wait and see are you all set?"

When they were set Jake tripped the wire a net came down and a loud noise sounded.

Six Indian's came running but no one caught in the net.

The Indians were too busy to notice the posse come up behind them.

The pose had them rounded up in no time at all and this lot were tied up.

Chad had half of the posse take them back to town and to jail.

"Well done Jake we would have all been caught if you were not here" Albert said gladly was.

Kate saw a rider coming towards them and said "hey guys we have a visitor" she pointed to the lone rider.

When he got close Chad saw that he had only one hand" this must be the man OldJoe told us about he is here to help.

Ethel was having a hard time with Monica. She wanted a drink she wanted something to eat and then there was the outhouse. Monica tried all kinds of things to get Ethel to untie her.

"Shut your mouth bitch or I'll carry out my son's order's" Ethel warned her

"Oh yeah and what would that be? You don't have what it take to inflict any more on me" Monica said with a smirk on her face. She thought Ethel was too timed for this kind of thing.

But she was wrong Ethel was in the kitchen heating up some small rocks over a wood fire as they did not have any coal but she thought this would do as good.

When Monica saw her drag a tin tray of hot rocks into the room she was scared.

It was as if she knew what Ethel was going to do with them.

Monica's face went bright red and she started to shiver shake and sweat started to run down her face.

Ethel put a wet towel over the rocks so steam came of them. She left the room and came back with a large pair of scissors.

Now Monica was really worried, what was she going to do with those scissors? She begged "Ethel please don't do this."

"Now who has the upper hand? Let's see who is the stronger's of the two of us" Ethel said like the power she had.

Ethel walked behind Monica grabbed her long black hair and cut her hair near the top of her head she said "There that's better you must feel a lot better now all that hair is gone."

All Monica could do was sit and cry she loved her long hair.

William rode up to Chad and the others stopped got of his horse and said. "Hi I've been expecting someone. You must be Chad the River View sheriff. I'm William Carter" he held out his hand out and shook Chad's hand.

After the introductions were over and William knew who everyone was they got down to planning how they were going to handle thing.

William told them he had Monica tied up at his house.

"Good work I don't know how you managed this and I don't think I want to know. But what I want to know is why you want to bring the outlaws to justice?"

William showed them his hand and then took off his boot he showed them what she did to his feet and said" It took me a very long time to get back to what you would say is near normal. They shot my father though the head for no reason at all just because he would not do as they said."

After what they saw and heard William they went to his mother's home.

Ethel had already cut Monica's boots she put her feet on the hot towel for few moments then took them off.

Monica was screaming in pain, but Ethel did not stop. She wanted Monica's feet to be just like Williams.

When Monica passed out with the pain, Ethel would grab her hair and pull her head back and then throw cold water on her face.

Monica did not come to "Ethel bent over her and said" No, no! don't you die on me now; we have just begun to get even."

As Ethel tried to bring Monica around she forgot that Monica's feet were still on the hot rocks. Suddenly Monica gave an almighty scream and tried to lift her feet, As she did the chair fell back and the wooden chair smashed in to pieces.

Monica got to her feet and hit Ethel over the head with a broken piece of the chair.

Then she took the rope and the remains of the chair and made her way back to her home just before William came home.

William came in and he saw his mother on the floor. "Mom what happen here?" he patted her face to bring her around.

Albert took the tray of hot stones outside and Kate took over for William, She had a cold cloth and started to wiped Ethel's face "Come on now you are safe your son is here" in a while Ethel came a round. The first thing she said was "where did that bitch go? Did she get away?"

"Yes mom she is gone but don't you worry about that I'm thankful you were not harmed."

Monica was sat in an easy chair after the doctor left.

She told a servant to go find her men. He came back with bad news saying. "I'm sorry but I could not find them, I looked everywhere I was been told they have not been around for a couple of days."

As the servant was telling her this, the men came up to the front porch, brushing dust off."

Yeah we have been out looking for you? What happen to you Phillip asked.

The men did not like what they saw. After hearing that Monica might loss one of her hands and it would take a long time before she could walk properly they decided to handle things until Monica was back in shape.

CHAPTER 8

Monica's Return

Jake knew they had failed again so they return to town.

On their way back they met wagon with a family from town with all their things "Sheriff you should know that a lot of people are leaving it is not safe anymore."

"But Mr Miller you and your family have lived here for many years what has made you do this?"

"Sheriff there was another killing while you were away so we are not staying to be murdered in our beds."

Chad did not like what he expected face when he got to town.

As they came into town they saw that a lot of people were on their way out.

At the jail the deputy was fast asleep in one of the cells. Chad called out, "Ned wake up you lazy bastard"

Jake and Albert sat in one of the office chairs. "What do we do now? Monica's men seem to be able to come and go anytime they want this is not good" Jake reminded Chad.

"Hey Jake you don't have to remind me that I have a lot of trouble. I'll get to the bottom of all of this trust me" Chad said angry that Jake thought he needed to remind him.

"Come on lads we don't need to be at each other's throat do we?"

They knew this sort of thing did not help so Chad said "No you are right Albert old boy as you English would say."

Chad had to talk to the undertaker about the woman who died.

Jake told Albert he was going back out there to talk to William and his mother.

"Do you think it is safe going out there without someone backing you up? So call me stupid but I'm going with you and no arguments"

"Yeah what about Kate? She won't like you being in danger again" Jake argued. "Well she will not know I'll be back before she comes back from seeing her Aunty. So no more talk we go."

Chad came back to the office after he found out t who was killed he said. "I'm glad you two are still here I need take the posse back out to William's place. I found out the woman who was killed was Anton's wife. This time we'll take a pack horse with everything we need. This might take a long time, but least we'll get a results."

Monica was laid up in bed and it was driving her mad. She could not get out to do what she wanted to do herself.

So she gave orders to her men and hoped they did not mess it up.

"This time you guys I want everyone to pay and that means pay with their lives. That bastard William is first then his mother. Then burn the house down don't let me down on this one" Monica ordered.

William and his mother were one step ahead of Monica hey knew she would be looking for revenge so they packed up their wagon left the night before.

William knew the wagon would not fit though the tunnel so they had to take the long way around.

They had to get past the lookout on top of the cliff but William knew the password to get past.

I t was a very long way going around and it took all night.

The next morning they were near the water fall but William knew his mother could not go further so he stopped to rest.

The sun was high in the sky when Ethel woke up and asked "Oh William is it late why did you let me sleep so long?" "Mom you needed the rest it's all right we are safe now."

No sooner he had said that than he saw dust fly up in the distance and he knew it came from a lot of horses.

He grabbed his rifle from the back of the wagon told his mother to stay put and hid behind some boulder s when they got close.

He saw the funny hat that Albert always wore he stood up behind the boulder and waved at them.

They stopped and Jake asked "what the hell are you doing out here?"

"long story pal come have some coffee and I'll bore you with the details"

Ethel had all ready started the coffee.

When Monica's men got to Williams house Sammy called out "Come out you worthless bastard or we'll burn your house down with you in it."

There was no answer

"alright you asked for it" he shouted as set fire to the house. They thought William and his mother were inside.

They left feeling good. They thought they had killed William and his mother.

They reported to Monica but she wanted to take revenge on the people of the town as well.

When Monica heard that William and his mother were dead and that the house was burned down to the ground.

Now she decided to burn down buildings in town as well.

After Chad and the others finished talking they went to Monica's camp.

Chad and his men went thought the tunnel and made rode what was left of William's house. "Chad it looks like Monica has had her revenge"

"Yeah the bitch is going all out I don't think she is going to stop there neither."

"Then it's time we paid her a visit. Let's see if we can't take her in and put her where she belongs"

As they got close to Monica's they heard a lot of screaming coming from the house.

Chad knocked on the door heard someone walk fast to the door and asked "Yeah what do you want?" an oversized woman asked.

"I would like to see Monica if she is at home"

"Yeah well you can't she is not here now. Go away" the woman said very angrily.

Jake and Albert went around the back to see if they could see in a window.

Luck was on their side as the back door was wide open. They went in being very quiet careful so no one saw them.

They went up stairs and heard talking in one of the larger rooms.

When they peeked they saw Monica sitting up in bed. The large woman sat on the side of the bed with her back to them. She seemed to be doing something to Monica's wrist.

They thought it best to get out of there fast before they were caught.

Chad and his men were waiting for Jake and Albert not far from the house

"Well what did you find out?"

"Chad you were right, She is in there, but she is laid up in bed, She has bandages on her wrist and her feet, This might be a good time to overpower her and take her in."

Monica had the feeling that she was being spied on and sent some Indians out to round up the intruders.

She told to lock them up in the barn for now. They surrounded Jake and Albert "Jake I don't think we will be overpowering anyone it looks like she has the upper hand now"

"Yes for now Albert."

Monica got a wheel-chair had her servant push her to the barn. "Well we meet again Jake. You have recovered from the last time you visited" she said with a smirk on her face.

"Your day will come you hard-hearted bitch" Jake said as he walked around looking for a way out.

Monica wheeled her chair close to Albert and said "I don't think we have had the pleasure I am Monica you may have heard of me"

"Yeah lady I have and I use the term lady loosely

"How nice you have an accent where are you from? You are not from around here?"

"If it is all any of your business I am from England and I am looking for one of your men"

"Which one would that be."

Albert got the signal to keep her talking while they found a way out.

But Monica had one eye on Albert and one eye Jake to make sure he did not find a way out.

"If you and your pal are thinking about getting out of this barn think again this time you are going to die here."

Monica's men were just coming to the Bentley farm" Sammy we were told to start burning down home. This is the first one I hope everyone is at home' Phillip laughed.

Harold threw a burning touch on the barn roof it went up in flames.

George came running out to put the flames out but he was gunned down.

His wife Heather ran out to him but it was too late. Phillip got hold of Heather and dragged her back in to the house.

Heather started kicking and screaming

"Be nice to me and I will let you live maybe"

"let me go you animal and get of four property"

"Now that is no way to talk to a person who hold your life in his hands." Phillip said as took Heather into a bed room and had what he called fun.

When he finished with her it was Harold's turn and then Sammy after they finished they shot her though the head.

They set the house on fire and ran the animals off they sat on their horses and watched.

Bret a young man on his way out of town saw the Bentley farm go up in flames.

He ran back to tell others in the town but he saw most of them packing their wagons.

The others just did not want to know.

The town's people were running scared with good reason.

Bret thought there must be something they could do to stop the outlaws.

He looked all over town for the deputy but he had left town as usual.

When things got a bit hairy the deputy got lost.

Bret saw many the people of Riverview go to the church for a meeting.

He followed them into the church where the priest stood in front.

Bret walked up to the front and said "I need to talk to you. We have to do something to protect ourselves"

The mayor stood up and asked" how do you propose to do this young man? These outlaws shot first and ask questions later. You only have to look sideways at them and they will shoot you clean though the heart."

Suddenly they heard the sound of gun fire outside. Everyone dropped to the floor to hide.

"look there are only three of them and a lot more of us. Who will stand with me" Bret said as he pulled gun and got behind a pews for protection.

The outlaws came into the church with guns blazing. Bret got a few rounds off but nowhere near his target.

Some of the town's people found a way out while others were gunned down the priest was shot and he lay dying on the altar.

Bret could do not more so he got out though a window the outlaws had shot out

Bret had to find Chad to get him to come back to town.

He knew that Old Joe might know where to find Chad.

Old Joe told him about the entrance to the valley behind the waterfall.

Jake kept looking for a way out but it seemed to be impossible task.

He walked to the back of the barn to test the boards in the back wall as they did not look very strong.

Then he saw Bret coming close to the barn.

Bret came to the back of the barn looked though the crack in the wall but he did not see anything or anyone.

By now the talk with Monica was finished and she went back to the house.

Jake waited till Monica was inside the house and said "Hey guys we have help Bret is here

"Not that young boy that has not yet begun to shave" Chad asked

"Well I don't care as long as we get out of here" Albert said and Jake agree.

Jake went to the back of the barn again to see if he could see where Bret went but could not see him.

Bret went to the front of the barn but did not get too close. He saw a guard standing in front of the door.

He rode further back behind some tree's Bret to think things though.

In town the outlaws blew the bank safe open only to find it was empty.

"If that don't beat all. The bank teller must have gotten here first the bastard left us nothing."

Sammy said walking around the bank shooting holes in the walls. "Come on Sammy, this is no good. We better make tracks" Phillip said as he started for the back door.

"Why? We have to finish what we were ordered to do or she won't like it"

"Harold, do you think I am going back to tell her that there was no money? She will think we are holding out on her.

"Yeah Harold this is where it all ends I'm with Phillip. Where are you headed?"

"I'm off to Canada. I have family there you are welcome if you want to come Sammy. You too if you want to come HaroldThe more the merrier."

Was this the last of the three outlaws or was there more to come.

After the outlaws left the town's people came out to see what they could salvage.

Bret could not figure out how to get the guard out of the way.

"That idiot will never get rid of that guard on his own" Chad said pacing. "Give him a chance he is only a boy" Jake tried to calm Chad down.

All was quiet for a while then a loud scream came from the house like someone was in great pain.

The guard ran to help and Bret unlocked the door

"About time now we can take that bitch in and put her where she can do no harm."

Chad was first to the house he went inside and up to Monica's room and then he stopped for a bit and listen.

The doctor was in there telling Monica that she may lose her right hand.

"You bastard! You take my hand off and I'll shoot you where you stand. You better think of something else", Monica shouted. She was angry and in a great deal of pain.

The doctor gave her something to make her sleep and said" That will keep her quiet for a few hours maybe I can save the hand" He was talking to someone in the room with him.

Chad signal to the others to come close to the door so they could over power the doctor and the large woman.

They let the doctor out and went in.

The doctor did not put a fight, he just stepped aside. The woman she tried to stop them from taking Monica but with all the guns drawn on her she gave up.

It was a long ways to town. About half way there Monica started to wake up but found she could not move.

They were not taking any chances and had tied her down to the wagon.

"Let me out of this you bastards"

"I'll make you sorry for this." She hollered as she tried to get out of her ties. She soon found that the more she twisted and turned the more it hurt.

When they reached the outskirts of town they were surprised to see town in such a mess. Monica said "Now you have nowhere to lock me up my men did a good job on your poor little town."

"Don't worry we'll think of something even if we have to lock you up with the animals." Chad warned her.

Chad got a room at the hotel that was not torched they locked Monica in it and nailed window shut so she could not get out that way.

William heard they had Monica in custody so he felt it was okay to take his mother back home to live where her family and friends were.

They went to take over Monica's house and Monica's little girl there by herself.

She was sitting in her mother's room crying

"Come to me I'll take care of you" said as she put her arms to the little girl.

Monica sat in her room wondering what happened to her men.

They were not much, but they were all she had. Suddenly she remembered her daughter Paula. She started calling out" Hey you out there hey you I need help

The guard the door a bit and asked "What is your problem?" You get that sheriff to come here it is important" tears started to roll down her face.

Chad did not want to go anywhere near her, but he had to. It was his job. "Yeah what is it that is so important?" "My daughter where is she? I left her at home. Please tell me she is all right." "Your daughter is being care for she is safe"

Please I need to see her can you bring her to me?" Monica was crying

Chad thought about this and decided he needed to talk to someone else about it.

He went to the priest to see if he could shed some light on it.

The priest told him it was not a good idea Paula was adopted and needed this time to settle down.

Chad did not like having to tell Monica that she could not see her daughter but did." You son-of-a bitch you lock me up here and now you tell me I can't see my daughter why?

This brought up the rest of bad news. He said" Monica you will never be able have anything to do with your daughter. She has been adopted to someone who will take good care of her."

This made Monica and again she pulled at her binding.

"Do you think you can do one thing for me?" "I'll try what is it"

"untie me"

"No" Damn untie me! You the window nail shut, the door has a guard on it and you know I can't get out of here. A woman need to do what she needs to do."

Chad did not want to argue any longer so he left.

The guard outside of the room got shock when he seen an oversize woman come down the hall.

"I am Thelma, Miss Monica's maid and I wish to see her now"

"Sorry ma'am but I have orders not to let anyone in to see her just now."

Thelma was in no mood to mess around with this little wimp so she smacked him with her arm and pushed him out of the way.

The guard lay on the floor out cold,

Thelma set about getting Monica out of there.

She had arranged a wagon to be below the window of Monica's room. Thelma wrapped a towel around her arm and smashed the glass pane out of the window. It was a long drop, so she tied Monica in a sheet and very slowly lowered her to the wagon. As Thelma was lowing Monica she kicked over a lamp.

It smashed into pieces and the oil went all over the floor. when Monica was safely in the wagon. Thelma left but as she was leaving she struck a match and threw it into the room.

It did not take long before the whole hotel went up in flames and it was too late to stop them they were long gone.

Thelma knew that Monica did not have any friend left in this part of the country so she took her to Mexico to her father's house in Mexico.

The End or is it

Foot note
 This is a small western I felt that it could get to boring if I made it any longer.